# Unlocked and Unlost

GABBI GREY

Kingston

I love being a locksmith. I help people fix their lives when things go awry. A badly sprained ankle has me laid up, but I dislike being idle, so a friend suggests I hire an assistant. Little do I know how truly chaotic my life is about to become. Although he's cute, it never occurs to me just how important he might become in my life.

Ethan

I've held a series of jobs since graduating from business college, but none has captured my attention. Assisting a grouchy locksmith proves to be one of the more interesting challenges. When I discover something truly astounding about him, my entire world view changes.

*Unlocked and Unlost* is an opposites attract, grumpy/sunshine, age gap, paranormal shifter gay romance with a stodgy racoon shifter and the glorious squirrel shifter fated mate he didn't see coming.

## Dedication

**Renae – I love your mind**

Copyright © 2025 Gabbi Grey.

All rights reserved.

No part of this book may be reproduced in any form or by any electronic or mechanical means, including information storage and retrieval systems, without written permission from the author, except for the use of brief quotations in a book review.

This is a work of fiction. Names, characters, places and incidents are either the products of the author's imagination, or are used fictitiously.

References to real people, events, organizations, establishments or locations are intended to provide a sense of authenticity and are used fictitiously. Any resemblance to actual events, locations, organizations, or persons living or dead is entirely coincidental.

NO AI/NO BOT. We do not consent to any Artificial Intelligence (AI), generative AI, large language model, machine learning, chatbot, or other automated analysis, generative process, or replication program to reproduce, mimic, remix, summarize, or otherwise replicate any part of this creative work, via any means: print, graphic, sculpture, multimedia, audio, or other medium. We support the right of humans to control their artistic works.

No generative AI was used in the creation of this book.

Edits by ELF

Cover by Jo Clement

# Contents

1. Chapter One — 1
2. Chapter Two — 11
3. Chapter Three — 22
4. Chapter Four — 33
5. Chapter Five — 44
6. Chapter Six — 56
7. Chapter Seven — 71
8. Chapter Eight — 85
9. Chapter Nine — 97
10. Chapter Ten — 105
11. Chapter Eleven — 118
12. Epilogue — 126
13. Interested in knowing more about Gabbi? — 133

# Chapter One

## Kingston

"Again, I can't tell you how sorry I am." Peter Erickson's wince came through the phone as clearly as if I was standing before the Academy Award-winning actor.

"Truly, Peter, I don't blame you. These things happen." I gazed at my wrapped ankle and tried to ignore the ache in my back.

"But..." He sighed. "If Skylar hadn't locked my keys in my filing cabinet—"

"Really—"

"And then you rushed here to unlock the cabinet because all my keys were in there."

"It's fine—"

"Skylar didn't mean to push her tricycle in your way just as you were stepping off the landing."

"I know." Which I did. The child never came across as a menace. She was just a curious three-year-old who liked mischief.

Or at least that's what Peter's husband Thomas maintained.

"When you went down...I saw it coming, and I couldn't get there in time."

Reliving the event wasn't doing anything to soothe my nerves. "It's not a big deal. You took me to the clinic to get my ankle wrapped. You and Thomas drove me and my van home. All's good."

"But now you can't work."

"Being a locksmith isn't generally impacted by a sore ankle." Of course the doctor had told me to keep all weight off it. Which really fucking sucked.

"But you can't drive. That's going to impact your income."

"I have insurance to cover things like this."

"But your business..." He sighed again—frustration truly evident.

"A few weeks off won't make a difference. I was due for a vacation anyway." Which was the European river cruise I'd planned for next month, but I wasn't going to tell him that. No sense adding to his guilt.

"Hey, Kingston, I know a guy. He needs a job. He just needs a break. He's a little...weird, but his heart's in the right place. He won't let you down. He'll drive you around and lift the stuff for you at work and home." Peter said the words in a manic rush. Almost like panic was encroaching.

"How do you know the guy?" Because, even with a recommendation from *the* Peter Erickson, I was still going to make this decision myself.

"He did some work for Thomas when I was down in LA for a couple of weeks last month. Between Thomas's schedule at the studio and the kids getting sick, he just needed someone. This guy's super reliable.

He'll be on time, take care of whatever you need, and everything will work out."

I wasn't really in a position to turn down assistance offered by Peter. I had helped people who worked at the studio a number of times over the years—including rescuing a fiery set designer and his straight-laced security husband who'd managed to get themselves locked in a closet. I hadn't asked questions.

Probably for the best.

"Fine. Send him over to my house. Ten tomorrow morning." I'd meet the guy and make the final determination myself. "Thank you for arranging this."

"You'll adore Ethan. Very...unique. Oh, sweetheart, let me—"

A crash sounded.

"Uh, Kingston?"

"Go. Thank you."

"Yeah." He cut the line.

Apparently, even award-winning actors had domestic issues. Kids were far beyond my expertise. I was pushing forty with a few close friends, no romantic partner, and zero prospects.

Which was fine with me.

I struggled to my feet and hobbled into my kitchen. I heated some ramen noodles in the microwave and ate them before the water had even softened them. I just wanted to get into bed, take an anti-inflammatory painkiller, and try to put this horrible day behind me. I wasn't a man who contemplated luck, but I'd have to admit tripping over a tricycle and twisting my ankle was pretty bad. The way I'd gone down had also pulled a muscle in my back.

Well, I supposed I was lucky that I hadn't injured either wrists or hands—that would've been catastrophic for my work. My hands were my weapons of war against the locks of the world. I saw this job as a vocation—a calling—as much as an actual paycheck.

With all that in mind, I was ready to go the next morning, wearing my crisp black uniform with my name in gray lettering. Fortunately, I owned ten identical outfits, so I wouldn't have to worry about washing anything for a bit of time. I might've been anal like that.

*Or lazy.*

Well, point taken.

My doorbell buzzed.

I shifted, reaching for my crutches.

The buzz sounded again.

I pushed myself off the couch.

*Buzz. Buzz. Buzz.*

I balanced myself.

More buzzes.

*Jesus, is he leaning on the buzzer? What is he, ten?*

Eventually, I struggled to the front door and threw it open.

The man who stood before me was just...a riot of red. Red shorts, red sneakers, red jaunty ball cap, and flaming red hair sticking out from underneath it. Hell, even his hairy legs were covered in red fuzz.

He wore a white T-shirt with a light-blue shirt over the top and was nearly bouncing on the spot. "Hey, dude. I'm Ethan. Great house you have here. I love the rosebushes out front. My gran has rosebushes. Uses lots of fertilizer on them. Bugger to prune. But I prune them for her. I could prune yours. And I love this area. Did you know Colin Firth lives around here? I dunno if it's true or not. I just heard it. But thanks for giving me a job. Peter said you needed help. I can help. Helping is great. What do you need help with? The roses? Your washing? Peter said something about driving. I can drive. Do you need to go now?"

I blinked.

Then I cleared my throat.

"Last I heard, Colin Firth lives in England. Somewhere near London, I think...?" Since I didn't keep track of random British celebrities, I couldn't be certain. "Maybe he was filming something in Vancouver." I wanted to scratch my scalp, but my grip on my crutches prevented that. "And yes, I could use a ride. I have a customer waiting." I managed to balance while pulling my keys out of my pants pocket.

"Oh great." He snagged them. "Which is your house key? This one?" He held one up.

I didn't even have the time to nod before he was closing the door and shoving the key in the lock. I winced, thinking of all the times I'd had to retrieve broken keys from locks.

"Perfect. Okay, so your van, right? Because you've obviously got all your work stuff in there. Is it armed? Do you worry about being broken into? Oh, you've got those surveillance signs. Warning people they're on camera. Which is super important for privacy but I figure everyone's got a camera, so if I scratch my ass, someone, somewhere, has it on video. But I see these signs and I wonder *is there really a camera, or is the sign just there to make me* think *there's a camera*? And I can see your doorbell cam, and does that cover your driveway as well, or do you have multiple—"

"Multiple. Shall we go?"

"Oh." His eyes widened. "Well, yeah, of course. I just didn't know if you needed anything from the garage—"

"Nope. We're good." With great effort, I descended the steps to the walkway, regretting the decision to buy a house with stairs. Classic Victorian design, but not the least bit accessible. If I'd wound up in a wheelchair for some reason, I would've been screwed.

Ethan had the passenger door open for me, which I grudgingly appreciated.

I managed to maneuver in, and he quickly grabbed my crutches—stowing them in the back. By the time I had my injured leg in the cab and the door closed, he was hopping into the driver's seat. He buckled his seatbelt, then turned to me expectantly.

"I'll program the GPS."

"Oh great." He turned the key in the ignition, and the engine purred to life.

I programmed the GPS.

"Turn left on Union Street."

"Holy shit." Ethan goggled at me. "Where'd you get that voice? I've never heard that voice."

"He's Australian." Because if I was going to spend my days driving around the lower mainland, at the very least, I was going to have a sexy Aussie dude giving me directions. "Uh, Ethan, we need to be leaving."

"Right." He grinned. "I love that you live in Strathcona. All the big old houses. And such history." He turned left on Union Street and headed west. "I live in Sunrise-Hastings. Lots of older homes, but without the character of yours. I mean, nothing wrong with the fifties, but the style is sort of all the same."

"Do you rent or own?"

He merged onto the Georgia Street Viaduct as per the GPS's instructions. "Own? Are you crazy? I'm twenty-four. Nah, I live with my parents. My goal is to move out by next year. Or maybe the year after. They live next to my gran, and I prune her roses, so I'd have to live close enough that I'd be able to visit to do her roses, and sometimes I mow her lawn as well." He veered around a slower-moving car.

Slower moving being relative—the startled woman was going five above the speed limit. "Traffic usually slows up ahead..."

"Oh, I know. That's fine, because I know a shortcut."

I frowned. Downtown Vancouver was in a grid pattern—it didn't have shortcuts. Even as I had the thought, he turned into an alley.

He squeezed past a garbage truck and tore down to the next street. I grabbed my door.

He turned onto Smithe Street and barreled toward the west end, turning despite a very yellow light. The light turned red before we were safely onto Howe Street.

*Don't say anything. You won't get a red-light ticket. There aren't any cops. You're grateful...remember that.*

Yet, as we ran at least ten klicks over the limit as we headed south, I needed to bite my tongue.

"So, I love Kerrisdale." He grinned. "Nice neighborhood with a mix of old and new houses. Do you know which one we're going to? Because, personally, I don't really care. I mean, I'd take anything. But I'll never be able to afford a place in Vancouver. Totally out of reach. So I'm looking at the suburbs. Like Coquitlam, Surrey, or even Abbotsford. Oh, or Mission City. I love Mission City with that monastery. It's just so pretty and—"

"Merge left onto Granville Street."

Ethan, bless his heart, followed the GPS's direction.

But that didn't slow him as he tore over the Granville Street Bridge, weaving in and out of traffic. "I like pretty, but I also like practical. Like, I need to find a full-time job. I've been trying out different things—figuring out what I might be good at. I haven't figured it out yet, but Gran says to be patient. That some people mature more slowly than others. How about you? Did you always want to be a locksmith? Because that's a pretty neat job—"

"Red-light camera ahead."

"Shit." Ethan eased off the gas as the light turned yellow. "Guess I won't run that one."

*Don't say anything. Don't say anything. Don't—*

"Do you always speed?"

"Oh, was I speeding? A cop friend of mine said you can go up to ten over the limit. Now, he got kicked off the police force for...well, the less said about that episode, the better. So maybe I shouldn't be following his advice? But he seemed like a stand-up guy. He's in private security now. He offered to get me a job with the company, but I couldn't imagine just sitting around doing nothing all day. Although some of their jobs involve driving from location to location, and I guess that would be okay. I mean, I'm a good driver. But I think that would get boring as well."

We climbed the hill heading south, and I winced. *We'll get out of this alive. We have to.*

Even as I had the thought, Ethan approached a driver who was turning right. Very slowly.

My new employee wove between two cars in the passing lane and then swerved back into the right lane with inches to spare.

"And I love the idea of trying new things, but I think I need to settle on something eventually, right? Right?" He met my gaze for a fraction of a second before looking back at the road.

*He has the most stunning bright-blue eyes. How had I not noticed them before?* "I'm sorry—what was the question?"

"Well, like, did you always know you wanted to be a locksmith? Was it some family tradition? Like, was your father a locksmith? Or did you just have this innate curiosity? I mean, you get to see what's in people's safes and shit like that. Which is enough to blow my fucking mind. Oh, you don't mind if I swear, do you? I promise I won't be around your clients, of course. But Peter said you were a chill guy.

Well, or something like that. And how cool is it that we both know Peter Erickson?" He hit the gas to fly through the intersection at West Twenty-Sixth just as a motorcycle was about to turn left in front of us.

The idiot, who didn't have the right of way, swerved.

To my sheer relief.

"They call motorcycle riders something like, uh, organ donors. That guy was an idiot. I mean, the light was green. I had the right of way. I might've been going a little fast, but not so much that it would make a difference. Man, if I'd hit him, I would've felt really bad. Like, I probably would've messed up your van—"

"Probably—"

"And that would've sucked. And the guy might've died or some shit, and that would've really been awful. And—"

"Family tradition."

"Huh?" He glanced over at me.

"Eyes on the road."

He sighed. "Well, duh."

To my relief, he faced forward again. "My father and grandfather were locksmiths. My grandfather came over as a young boy from Ukraine after the First World War. Most of the immigrants at that time chose an agrarian homestead, but we came all the way across the country. My great-grandfather had a farm in Cedar Valley, but he insisted his eldest son learn a trade. My grandfather chose locksmith and moved to Vancouver. He and my grandmother settled and had my father. He, in turn, married my mother, and they had me. I apprenticed with him and took over the business when he retired. My parents passed a few years ago after having lived into their seventies."

See? I could totally rival his blathering on, and that was probably the most I'd said to anyone in...well, as long as I could remember.

"So you're Ukrainian?"

"Well, my heritage is. I'm Canadian."

"So what's going on...?"

"Makes me very sad. And I send money to several aid organizations—"

"Turn right on West Forty-Ninth Avenue."

*Holy crap, I talked for like fifteen blocks.* "And yes, it's cool we both know Peter Erickson. I understand you were very helpful to his husband, Thomas."

"I was. My friend Seamus works with Thomas, and when Thomas seemed overwhelmed, Seamus suggested Thomas hire me to help out. Seamus used to live near me. And he works at the studio as well. As a production assistant. And he's married to this super gorgeous man named Valentino. I've met him a couple of times. He's a bigshot executive, and I sort of find him intimidating, and I can't figure out if that's because he's so handsome or just, you know, his status. I've only met Peter once, and he's super gorgeous, but I didn't find him as intimidating. Which, given he's an Academy Award-winning actor, would mean I should've been more intimidated—"

"Turn left on Balsam Street."

Ethan, to my relief, managed to do just that.

"I try not to be intimidated by my clients." *If I keep him in the van, maybe he won't recognize my client... Except I need him to carry in my equipment.*

*Fuck.*

*This isn't going to end well.*

# Chapter Two

Ethan

"887 Balsam Street is on your right." Sexy Australian voice again.

I eased the van onto the driveway and came up to the closed iron-barred gate. "Uh, who did you say your client is?"

"I didn't." Kingston pursed his lips.

"So do I enter a code, buzz, or—" Before I was able to finish the question, the gate swung open. "Wow, that's cool."

"Thornton was expecting us. We were just..." He checked his watch. "Well, we're early."

"Oops." *I didn't drive that fast, did I?*

I pulled up to the house, put the van in park, and cut the engine. "Electric sure is sweet. So good for the environment. Especially because we have hydro power, which is a clean form of electricity. I mean,

I don't necessarily understand how all that powerful water up north delivers electricity for my stove, but I'm super... Holy hell."

"Try to stay cool, okay? No...gawking." Kingston opened the door, then banged his foot against it when he tried to get out.

I leapt into action. I had my seatbelt off and scurried about to his side of the van in time to hand him the crutches and to help him out.

By then, the blond god had come around to greet us. "Good God, Kingston, what happened? You should've told me. This absolutely could've waited a week or two." He eyed the wrapped ankle. "Or six."

"I would've tried to tell him that, but he wasn't likely to listen to me, and since my job is to take care of him as best I can, without arguing too much, I figured I'd just bring him here and, well, you know. And it's lovely to meet you. I'm Ethan, and you know Kingston, of course. Best locksmith in town." I puffed out my chest. Then considered my words—something I rarely did after they'd left my mouth. "Okay, I don't *know* he's the best, but he did work for Peter Erickson, and I'm guessing Peter wouldn't hire anyone but the best. Although he hired me. So does that mean I'm the best or was just the most convenient? Because I have a lot of free time—"

"I wonder why..." Kingston muttered the words.

Likely he'd thought he spoke under his breath, but I had super-sensitive hearing.

The blond god smiled. "I'm Thornton. It's nice to meet you, Ethan."

He didn't offer to shake my hand, but I wasn't offended by that.

He pivoted to Kingston. "Are you certain you're up for this?"

My new boss nodded.

"Something to keep me busy." He eyed me. "Otherwise, I might lose my mind."

I was *not* going to take offense at the inference that I'd cause him to lose his mind.

Or was I?

Was that what he'd meant?

*Sometimes you don't have the sense God gave you. Just hush now.* My father's words echoed in my head. He'd never been my biggest supporter. That's why I was so lucky I had Gran. "Do you need equipment?"

"Yes." Kingston's dark gaze settled on me. "The gray tool kit." He turned to Thornton. "Wall safe?"

Thornton nodded. "We didn't even know the damn thing was there. Ed knocked over a drink, and while he was cleaning, he noticed the liquid was traveling in an unexpected direction. We followed it and found a false panel in the wall. Damn curious, and having already decided the olive-colored seventies wallpaper had to go, we hired a construction crew to take apart the wall. Go figure. The specs of the house did *not* show an entire antechamber. In retrospect, the space was unaccounted for, but, you know..."

"Your house is so big it doesn't matter?" I chuckled. "Because, no offense, you've got a big house. I mean, I don't know what I'd do with that much space. Well, I suppose I would get my gran to move in. She'd know what to do. I mean, she always knows what to do. Grans are smart that way. Do you have a gran? Well, that's a stupid question, because everyone has grandparents, but I guess I'm asking if you've got a special grandparent in your life..."

His sad expression had me trailing off.

He offered a smile after blinking several times. "My grandfather. He loved photography, and he instilled that love in me. Instead of becoming a doctor or lawyer, I became a documentary filmmaker."

"Oh." I perked up. Well perked up more. "Have you done something I've heard of? I mean, I don't watch many documentaries. Nature ones, for certain."

"You know, I'm mostly known for my documentary about a rock band, but I did one on the mating habits of elk."

I blinked. "And bull moose? Oh my God, that's a favorite of mine. I watch it all the time. Have you ever considered doing one about squirrels? Specifically squirrels in an urban environment? I don't think there are enough shows about how nature and humans interact—"

"Everything okay out here?" A stunning Black man with dreads stepped out from the house. Despite the chilly autumn afternoon, he had bare feet, ripped jeans that hugged his hips in just *that* way, and a tight T-shirt. He was shorter than the blond god, and... "Holy shit, you're Ed Markham."

He blinked. Then seemed to recover himself. "Uh, yes, yes, I am. I don't think we've met."

"Well, of course we haven't met. Because you're Ed Freaking Markham and I'm just little old Ethan who *can't get his shit together* as my father likes to say."

"But he's helping me today, so he's going to have to get his shit together." Kingston glared. "My ankle is killing me."

"Oh crap." I scurried around to the back of the van, but not before I heard him say, "No, I'm fine. I just don't know where his off-switch is. Apologies."

I should've felt hurt, but I kind of didn't, because hell, even I knew I could be a little much. I retrieved the gray tool kit, slammed and then locked the door, and headed back.

Ed had returned to the house, and Kingston was being escorted by—

"You're Thornton Graves." The pieces were coming into place. *That* documentary about *that* rock band. Grindstone.

He offered me a smile. "The name my mother calls me. Although I think Markham-Graves has a better ring to it."

"Married, eh?" Kingston grinned. "That's great."

Thornton sighed. "Yeah, it is. We both have professional credits, though, so hyphenating names—or taking each other's—"

"I'm more than willing to ditch Markham." Ed poked his head out of the house. "I'm not attached to mine like you are to yours."

"I didn't mean—"

"Your family's amazing. Mine fucking sucked. Doesn't seem like much of a debate to me." He puffed out his chest. "I think Ed Graves is perfect."

Thornton cleared his throat. "I don't think we need to discuss—"

"Yes, we do. Our friends should help us settle this."

"We have a big house because when Grindstone is recording their next album, everyone wants to be in the same place. We're kitting out the recording studio in the back." Thornton was clearly not interested in having the last-name discussion and picked up on a comment I made earlier.

"Yes, this place used to belong to music producer—"

Thornton cleared his throat.

Ed laughed. "Right. Sorry. You don't need to hear about all this." He gestured to Kingston. "It's not too far. I'll get a chair for you. This secret room is pretty cool."

Did people say *cool* anymore? I wasn't certain. Ed didn't seem that much older than me. Well, neither did Thornton, for that matter. Certainly, we were all younger than the rather stodgy Kingston.

*Stodgy can be sexy.*

Yeah, it really could.

I stepped out of my sneakers and bent to help Kingston out of his shoes.

He glared.

Thornton laughed. "No, you can totally wear your shoes in the house. It's going to be messy once we start the construction. We thought we were happy with things the way they were, but between the discovery of the wall safe and the realization we really can't live with drab-olive wallpaper..."

Ed tucked himself into Thorton's side. "But the studio has to be finished first. Our record label is planning a big tour for us next year, and we need an album first. Our drummer Meg and her husband Big Mac just had their first child—"

"Which Big Mac swears is going to be their only."

The two men looked at each other and laughed.

We followed them out of the grand foyer, through the living room, on through the dining room, and to a large living space with floor-to-ceiling windows looking out over a magical garden.

"It must be so beautiful in the summer." I stepped toward the glass. Even on this dull, gray day, the light illuminated the space.

"We have a gardener who will take care of all of that." Ed grinned.

"Yeah, we've seen the pictures. Can't wait."

"Okay, and why did you laugh when you said *Big Mac swears this is going to be their only...*?"

"Ethan." Kingston held a warning tone in his voice.

"You need to sit." Thorton drew our attention to a little alcove.

Immediately, I saw why they hadn't noticed. The antechamber was next to the fireplace and just appeared to be flush with it. But on the other side, the bookshelf was set back. When one looked hard enough, the difference was clear. But one had to be looking.

# UNLOCKED AND UNLOST

Thornton ushered Kingston to a chair Ed must've placed there. Then he turned to me. "The birth wasn't easy on Meg. Big Mac doesn't ever want to see his wife go through that again."

"But Meg wants at least one more." Ed grinned. "And I have to say that what Meg wants, she gets."

"I find that's usually smartest." I placed Kingston's tool kit next to him and opened it.

He glared.

I smiled.

He turned back to the wall safe.

I pivoted to the men. "Like my gran says, arguing with a lady is really rude. I mean, if the lady's wrong and someone might get hurt, that's one thing. But arguing for the sake of arguing? That's just..." I scrunched my nose. "Although I guess you could say that arguing with anyone just for the sake of arguing is wrong. But my dad's like that. He'll take the opposite view from me—even if he's never felt that way before.

"And I don't know if it's, like, to toughen me up or to make me defend my positions. Sometimes I can see I'm wrong. I will totally admit that. Because admitting being wrong is a sign of strength. Or at least that's what gran says. She says toxic masculinity is real and I have to always be gentle with everyone, especially—"

"I've got it open."

That brought me up short. For some reason, I'd assumed it would take Kingston, like, hours to open the safe. Not a mere... I checked my watch. Eight minutes.

"Perfect. Okay, what's in it?" Ed moved closer.

Kingston swung open the door.

Thornton and I inched closer as well.

"Well, I'll be damned." Ed cocked his head. "Is that... a stamp collection?"

Several stamps were displayed in frames while there were stacks and stacks and stacks of books.

Ed snagged one and opened it. "Oh, wow." He passed it to Thornton and grabbed another one.

Thornton opened it and showed me.

Beautiful, vibrant postage stamps.

I burst out laughing. "All that for this?"

Thornton grinned. "Totally worth it. Plus, we're getting rid of that wallpaper."

For the first time, I really looked. I moved to the wall and ran my hand along the raised section. It felt...fuzzy. "What the hell?"

"Very 1970s." Ed laughed. "We've been busy since we moved in. There's a massive room in the basement, and we hang out there with the band. This room's been a low priority. Would you like a tour of the house? Kingston's seen it all since he re-keyed everything here for us."

"Wow, that must've been a lot of work." I scrunched my nose as I tried to figure out how many locks would actually be involved.

"Actually, he's very efficient." Ed patted Kingston on the back. "Would you like a coffee while Thornton shows your friend around? Oh, or do you have somewhere else to be? We don't want to hold you up."

*Please don't have somewhere else to be. Please say* yes *to the coffee. Please—*

"Tea would be lovely, if you don't mind."

"Tea's great. I'm going to have another coffee because Axel is coming—"

"Axel Townsend is coming here?" Okay, I might've squeaked that. Ed was Grindstone's bassist, and totally hot. But Axel? The lead singer? When he took his shirt off, crowds went nuts.

Kingston sighed as he maneuvered himself onto his crutches. He met Ed's gaze. "Don't mind him. He's...new."

Ed laughed. "As opposed to you who've been catering to the whims of Vancouver's elite for years. Oh, the secrets you know."

"And will never share." He eyed me. "Like today."

I nodded. Keeping my mouth shut about today would be like, *super* hard, but I'd do it. I hadn't told anyone about Peter and Thomas. Well, Gran knew. And she'd reminded me to keep my mouth shut if I wanted to work for them again in the future. I mimed zipping my lips.

"While I'm making the tea, I'm going to text the realtor, Juanita. She'll have to figure out how to get the stamps to the next of kin."

I cocked my head.

"Oh, the music producer died." Thornton shrugged. "Died in the primary bedroom. So we got a bit of a deal on the house."

Connecting those two thoughts took me a moment. I wasn't suspicious. If someone died, they died. Where and how didn't really matter to me.

"Let's get started on the tour. We'll head upstairs."

Forty-five minutes later, Thornton and I left the studio and headed back to the main house, walking past the pool. "This is so very cool." Okay, apparently I said *cool* sometimes.

Thorton shrugged. "I inherited a nice sum of money and sold my loft in Portland. The documentary reached a decent audience, and...I probably shouldn't be sharing all my secrets."

Again, I mimed zipping my lips. For some reason, people found me easy to talk to. Which was awesome because I discovered lots of neat little facts, but sucked because I had to keep those secrets inside me, even as they wanted to burst from my chest.

Kingston and Ed sat at the breakfast table, again with the stunning view of the backyard, with a stack of about twenty of those stamp collection books on the table.

Ed shrugged. "They're now ours. Juanita spoke with the producer's son, and the guy made it clear he didn't want anything to do with it. I said we should pay, and the guy said to enjoy our discovery. Juanita interpreted that as *fuck off, I'm good*. Who are we to argue?"

"What are we going to do with them?"

"I thought..." He cleared his throat. "This is something you pass down through generations, right? And with Meg and Big Mac having kids..."

I wanted to ask if these two planned to have children. Or Axel with his husband Hugo. But that was *way* beyond what would be considered proper.

Even I knew that.

"So we put them back in the safe—only we'll have the combination this time—and in twenty years we see if there is a child in our lives who is interested." Thornton laid his hand on the pile gently.

"Sounds logical." Ed held out his hand.

Thornton grasped it.

The moment held suspended.

"So, like, does anyone want peanuts?" I reached into the pocket of my pants and yanked out a package of salted peanuts. "Because I'm really hungry, and I'm always happy to share." Truthfully, I could've eaten the entire pack, but I was trying to be polite.

"We'll let these good men get on with their day, and we'll eat something at my—" Even as Kingston said the words, his phone buzzed. "Pardon me."

Thornton grinned. "I love peanuts."

Taking that as permission, I ripped the package open.

Both Thornton and Ed happily took a handful.

As much as I wanted to scarf down the rest, I knew better. I saved a couple for Kingston, but the glare he gave me had me changing my mind and downing the rest of the package myself.

I was about to pocket the wrapper when Thornton snagged it from me. With a grin. "Least we can do. We're in your debt. Maybe you'd like to come by another day to meet the band?"

"Oh, that would be—"

"Completely unnecessary." Kingston struggled with his crutches.

I would've offered to help, but somehow I sensed that wouldn't be welcomed. Instead, I bent to pick up the tool kit—which Ed had clearly carried in here.

"We need to be going. I just got another callout." He met my gaze. "This is a specialized call, and so we're driving out to Cedar Valley. You need to be somewhere else?"

"No. Peter said I'm to stick with you until you can take care of yourself. You won't be able to get rid of me."

"God help me."

Thornton and Ed laughed.

Kingston didn't.

# Chapter Three

Kingston

The drive to Cedar Valley was uneventful. Ethan followed the directions from my very sexy Aussie GPS voice along the Number 7 highway all the way to Mission City. As expected, instead of being directed to the main strip, the voice instructed us to go up into the hills north of the town.

We turned onto a driveway that went several hundred feet before emerging into a clearing with an imposing mansion.

Ethan gasped. "Oh wow."

"No one famous this time." I eyed him. "Were the three packs of peanuts enough? This should also be a fairly quick job." I didn't want him begging for food. He was...unpredictable. And we probably should've stopped for something to eat, but I'd wanted to get here as quickly as possible. Nothing urgent, but my reputation of being prompt meant if I could go, then I went.

He batted his eyelashes. "I can work with deprivation."

"People far more deprived than you are out there."

"Right." He bit his lip, apparently taking to heart my chastisement.

I shouldn't have, though. Maybe, at one point in his life, he'd been deprived. Hell, maybe he was now. I didn't know enough about him to be making grand assumptions like he had enough to eat.

Before I could say anything, he hopped out of the van, grabbed my crutches, and brought them to me.

I grunted in appreciation.

"Hello." A young woman with her dark hair pulled into a ponytail came out to greet us, waving. A dog who appeared to be a husky followed at her heels.

Ethan knelt and held out his hand. "Oh sorry, is this okay? I just love dogs."

She laughed. "It's fine. Whalley, say *hi*."

The dog approached him with what I'd say was caution. He sniffed Ethan's hand, then backed away, his eyes wide.

*Oh shit, right.* That didn't look good.

Then he backed up and lunged at my smaller companion.

Ethan caught him, but with an obvious effort.

The dog was *big*. I didn't know much about dogs, but I guess seventy or eighty pounds.

"Oh, Whalley." The young woman moaned.

"It's fine." Ethan managed to get the words out between all the licks the pooch was delivering. Seemed he wanted to lick every inch of bare skin he could reach. "Uh, does he chase squirrels?"

She cocked her head. "Yes. But he wants to play with them. It's the weirdest fetish."

*Interesting choice of word.*

"You're Tarah Merrick?" I glared at Ethan. Enough blathering on about squirrels.

He gripped Whalley tighter to him. Almost like he was worried I might do something like insist he let the damn dog go.

"Yes, that's me. Sebastian's taking an emergency phone call. Uh, Dante recommended you."

"He did." I strove to remain neutral. Dante ran the most exclusive BDSM club in all of Vancouver. He'd needed my services a few times over the years—usually involving handcuffs, manacles, and door locks. Amazing the creative things BDSM folks could get into.

"Right. So you're aware..."

"Tarah, there pretty much isn't anything I haven't seen in my more than twenty years of doing this."

"How old are you?"

"I was going out with my daddy by the time I could walk. Learned from the best." I tipped my head. "Including discretion."

She laughed, with her bright-blue eyes sparkling. "Well, that's a relief. We...hesitated."

"Never with me. Whatever I see here will follow me to the grave."

"Unless it involves the safety of children. I know." She nodded. "I'm a teacher. I get it."

"Oh, what age of kids do you work with?" Ethan grinned. "I love kids. I mean, most of the time, I feel like one, which is probably why they like me. Kids and dogs. Everyone in my neighborhood knows me, so I can hang out at the park, and people don't think it's weird, and all the kids and dogs know me. So many friends. But it's hard that the kids grow up and then stop coming to the park, and I'll see them later riding their bikes or even driving cars and I feel sort of sad."

I stared down at him.

He still clung to the damn dog.

"You're twenty-four. How does that math work?"

He squinted as if trying to discern my meaning.

"Why don't you come inside. Is this young man your apprentice?" Tarah snapped her fingers, and Whalley disentangled himself from Ethan and came to his owner's side.

I cleared my throat. "Uh, not my apprentice." *More like a pain in my ass.* "He can be discreet as well. Unfortunately, I need him to carry my bag."

Ethan huffed.

Lucky for him, Tarah didn't appear to hear. We were going to have words.

I waited until he returned with my bag, and then we made our way into the house. The grandeur from the outside very much carried on into the inside. The soaring two-story foyer had massive windows with a stunning view of the trees between the house and the road, affording a great amount of privacy.

Again, Ethan toed off his shoes and then helped me remove mine.

"Oh, I'm so sorry." Tarah winced. "And the, uh, door is downstairs. Oh, I wish I could somehow bring it up to you."

Which was an adorable and completely impossible idea. "It's fine. I'll manage."

"I'll go right before him so if he trips, he lands on me." Ethan grinned.

I groaned. "You'll do no such thing. There will be no tripping. Stairs aren't a big deal."

He arched an eyebrow, undoubtedly holding back a snarky comment about how unsteady I still was on the fucking crutches. Well, I'd made it nearly forty years without ever having needed the damn things. Not my fault. And I was getting better.

Slowly.

Tarah pointed to a door. "It's down here."

"Sweetheart?" An attractive, tall man stepped out from a hallway. He spotted Ethan and me a fraction of a moment later. He frowned. "Are you okay?" Clearly the question was directed at me.

"My apprentice will help. Although if you could put a chair before the door so I can sit while I work, I'd appreciate it."

"Absolutely." He opened the door Tarah'd pointed to and disappeared.

Ethan gestured for her to go first.

She disappeared.

He eyed me.

I scowled.

"Well, I'm going to stand at the bottom of the stairs. Just don't trip." With that little quip, he headed down.

I drew in a deep breath, said a prayer, and approached the stairs with trepidation.

In the end, I was able to get down without falling. Came close twice, but managed to steady myself.

Ethan's blue eyes glinted amusement in the low light of the hallway.

Tarah pointed to a door on the left. "That's the entertainment room. Big-screen television, reclining chairs, pool table, area for the kids to play…" She pointed to the door on the right. "And that's the playroom."

Ethan frowned. "Your kids have two playrooms? Oh God, that's just so much fun."

Sebastian, who stood behind Tarah—with a hand at the small of her back—coughed. He caught my gaze.

"Apprentice." I tried to keep my voice level. "I, uh, didn't…" *What's the right answer to this? That I don't trust him? Except I'm starting to...* At the very least, he hadn't told Tarah about meeting Ed from Grindstone—even though I'd half expected him to.

Tarah covered her mouth, obviously smothering a laugh.

Fatigue and aching pits had me easing onto the stool. I appreciated Sebastian had selected something that put me at eye level with the broken deadbolt.

Ethan was there to position my tool kit and to relieve me of the crutches.

"Thank you." A bit harder to say than it should've been, but the little guy was getting on my nerves for reasons I couldn't articulate.

"Would you like something to drink?" Sebastian eyed the lock. "Or would you like to be left in peace?"

"Oh, he doesn't mind if we talk. Because, like, I have to tell you how pretty your house is. I mean, you don't even have olive-green bumpy wallpaper or anything. Oh, but, do you have a pool? The last house had a pool. And it's too cold to swim now, obviously, but like in the summer I think it would be so amazing to swim. And, like, even if you don't have a pool, you have trees. So many pretty trees. My neighborhood has old trees too, but not as tall as yours. Oh, I'd love to climb your trees."

With every word he spoke, my shoulders hunched more and more. Surely I had enough money to live on while I healed.

*Yes, but people need you. Tarah and Sebastian would've hesitated to call just any locksmith, despite the fact most wouldn't judge.* Judgmental locksmiths didn't get repeat business. The idea of missing calls because of a fucking twisted ankle was more than I could bear. So I'd put up with Mister Verbal Diarrhea and somehow not kill him.

But it'd be the biggest challenge of my life.

Of that, I had no doubt.

"If Kingston doesn't need you, perhaps you'd like to take a walk with me to see the trees?" Tarah beamed. "You can't climb them—liability and all that—but you're certainly free to look around. But only if—"

"Kingston can absolutely cope. If you don't mind showing him around..."

She grinned, looped her arm in Ethan's, and guided him back up the stairs.

I let out a long breath.

"Apprentice?" Sebastian's amusement was clear. "Dante didn't mention him."

"Oh God, please don't mention him to Dante. He's...temporary." I pointed to the crutches.

"We could've called someone else. Just I mentioned the, uh, problem to my friend Smith, who happens to own Club Kink. He mentioned it to Dante, and the next thing I knew, I had your number, and I was texting."

"I'm glad you did." I eyed the lock. "Whoever installed this did a piss-poor job. Oh, sorry." I didn't normally swear, but between my ankle and my new companion, I was completely discombobulated.

Sebastian laughed. "Not an issue here, my friend. All good."

I sorted through my tools before finding the one I needed. "But it's going to take a bit of time for me to remove and then replace the lock. I'm assuming that's what you want?"

"Oh hell, yes." He coughed. "Don't want some random young one wandering in there. Not that many of my friends don't have ones of their own..."

"Still." I squinted.

"Yeah. My honorary niece, Cara, has figured out door handles and is a damn curious child. She's going to be hell on wheels, and her baby brother likely will be as well. Not to mention..." He waved me off. "Lots of kids happening."

"You and Tarah?" I winced. "Sorry, normally I'm much more circumspect."

"That's okay." He chuckled. "Planned. She's still in teacher's college, though. That said, I'm not getting any younger."

I didn't figure the guy was more than a year or two older than me. Hell, maybe even the same age or younger. We both had black hair. Maybe with a bit of gray at the temples, although I'd never own that. But while his eyes were a dark inscrutable brown, mine were gray. "You'll work it out. I'm not going to say anyone's too old since my dad was forty-two when he had me. Just hadn't found the right woman. Perpetual bachelor. I think my grandmother despaired of ever having grandchildren, and my grandfather, who was all about upholding traditions, wanted someone to follow in their footsteps."

"As a locksmith."

"As a locksmith." I caught the bolt as it slid out. "Would you mind...?"

"Happy to help." He grabbed everything from me. "Seems a waste to throw this out. I knew that guy was trouble. Just...you know how you get a feeling?"

"I do." I rummaged in my kit for the new bolt. Since I didn't know who had helped Sebastian initially, I wasn't going to comment.

Well, I wouldn't have, even if I had known the guy.

"He kept asking all these questions about why we needed a deadbolt. He kept joking we were going to carve up dead bodies." Sebastian scratched his stubbled jaw. "Tarah took off, and he started making derogatory comments about women. I was like, buddy, read the room. I love my wife. Would do anything for her. You disparaging women does you zero favors in this place. Just because she's noticeably younger than me, doesn't mean I don't respect her greatly."

"I can see that. I know what you mean." I didn't have any patience for misogynists. Occasionally I'd discover I had one for a client. I'd finish the job, walk away, and never go back. Same with racists. I'd rather go hungry than work for assholes like that. Usually men, but not always.

"Can you help me with this?" *Should've asked Ethan to stick around. Less awkward to ask a theoretical employee than a client.*

*Wait.*

*What am I paying him?*

Another question I hadn't bothered to ask. Was he a proper employee? I'd never had one of those since I preferred to work for, and by, myself. I didn't have a storefront—my entire business model relied on me coming to the people who needed my service. When I was no longer able to do that, I'd retire. Sell my equipment to someone else and enjoy my salad days.

Hopefully it would be a long time from now.

"Happy to help." Sebastian moved to assist me, and thirty minutes later, he carried my tool kit up the stairs with ease while I struggled mightily.

*It's going to be a long fucking six weeks.*

Chattering drew my attention.

Sebastian placed my equipment by the front door, then gestured toward the back of the house with his chin. "Do you want to come with me, or should I simply let him know you're ready to go?"

Although intensely curious about what my chatty assistant was saying, my ankle throbbed. "I think we need to get going."

"Right. I'll get him. Bank transfer okay? Or would you prefer cash? I think I might even have a checkbook around here somewhere.

Tarah's on me about organizing my home office. Just so much to do...."

Including, as he'd casually pointed out, spending a fair amount of time in his BDSM dungeon—which they referred to as their *playroom*.

*Not going to explain that one to Ethan. Probably a good thing he was out looking at trees by the time I got the door fixed.*

"Bank transfer is perfect. Thank you."

"Oh, there you are!"

Before Sebastian even had a chance to head toward the kitchen, Ethan came barreling from that direction. "Tarah offered to cook, but I said you wouldn't want to impose. I was right, right? Because if I'm wrong, she said she's got a great teriyaki chicken recipe, and—"

Sebastian groaned.

Tarah, who'd followed excited Ethan, poked her husband in the ribs. "That was *one* time."

"Well, you are memorable. I'll never forget the state of my kitchen—"

She poked him again.

He laughed. And turned to me. "She makes a mean chicken teriyaki for certain. And you're welcome to stay. It's almost dinnertime, and you came all this way."

"It's okay, we need to be going."

"But I'm hungry." Somehow, Ethan managed to elongate the word and sound like a whiny two-year-old.

"We'll stop for some food."

"Oh, you should try Fifties. The diner isn't exactly on your way back to Vancouver, but it's worth the little detour." Tarah laced her arm in her husband's. "Best burgers in Cedar Valley. Well, best I've ever had. Although I haven't been many places—"

"Which we'll rectify when you're finished your studies." Sebastian gave her a fond smile. Then turned his attention back to Ethan and me. "Their Monte Cristo sandwich is amazing, and the barbecue chicken wrap is good as well. If you're trying to avoid the heavy stuff."

Ethan vibrated. "Oh, heavy sounds heavenly. I'm so—"

"Hungry, yes, I got the message." I glanced over at him. "If you wouldn't mind taking the tool kit out to the van?"

I'd barely uttered the words before he was off like a shot.

Tarah laughed. "I'll go keep him company."

"You mean supervise."

She cocked her head. "I find him charming." She pressed a kiss to Sebastian's cheek. "Back in a few." She followed Ethan and, apparently, the dog who'd taken off after him.

"You know…" Sebastian followed me as I headed toward the front door. "My wife's not easily charmed, and my dog's a rescue who'd been abused and doesn't trust easily. Your *assistant* seems to have wooed both."

I met his gaze.

He shrugged. "I'm just saying there are worse things in the world than to be surrounded by that much joy. Something to think about."

# Chapter Four

Ethan

I opted for the burger. With a garden salad instead of fries. I almost ordered a side of beer-battered onion rings, but then I remembered I wasn't paying for this meal. Nope. Kingston had spent five minutes in the van explaining how he was feeding me since obviously missing a meal had made me a little loopy.

Something about climbing trees.

To me, the urge to climb tall, beautiful oak trees was perfectly rational. All those sturdy branches. Hundred-or-more-year-old trees. An absolute delight for me.

Tarah had tempered my enthusiasm by explaining that property insurance probably wouldn't cover any accident. And that she wouldn't have thought of such things before becoming a teacher and learning how to care for ten-year-olds. Well, almost a teacher. I just admired her for being willing to do such a tough job.

I'd considered teaching. But that would've meant university for at least six years. My mind didn't work that way. I'd managed a two-year program in business. Lots of math, which my brain didn't like either. The creative stuff like marketing and public relations had been far more interesting for me.

Putting my learning to use was tough. Instead, I'd flitted from gig to gig, always keeping myself busy.

"How's your food tasting?" The server, with a nametag that read *Sarabeth* offered us a wide smile. She had the prettiest bright-blue eyes.

They reminded me of Tarah's.

Kingston's mouth was full of strawberry waffles—with extra whipped cream—so I offered a smile back. "Everything's perfect. This place is charming." The walls of the diner were covered in posters. Pinup girls, '50s muscle cars, as well as other Canadiana things. Very Mission City, I was discovering.

Sarabeth waved, then headed back to the front of the restaurant.

Kingston grunted.

I grinned. "I swear they time it so you've got your mouth full and all you can do is nod and give a thumbs-up."

He scowled. With Sarabeth's permission, we occupied one of the bigger booths, and Kingston had his leg lying along it, with him squished against the wall because he was so tall. His leg was long, and he didn't want it hanging over the edge where someone might jostle it.

I would've been okay with taking him straight home, but he insisted I needed a proper meal.

He probably hadn't anticipated me slathering peanut butter on my burger instead of ketchup.

What could I say? I liked what I liked, and judgmental, grumpy locksmiths could just lump it.

Which just made me happier.

The grumpier he got, the more I smiled. Not to annoy him, of course, but to make him...more confused.

Gran always said to meet dourness with kindness. That the more I smiled, the greater my impact on the world.

I'd taken that advice with me to the six-month contract I'd had at the tax department, answering phone calls. The more distressed the caller, the more I tried to smile. That hadn't always worked. When the contract ended, I didn't try to get another one. Too depressing.

"The food is delicious." Kingston wiped his lips. "The whipped cream is exceptional."

"High praise, coming from you."

He scowled again.

I giggled.

"From the man who puts peanut butter on hamburgers. And carries around packages of peanuts in his pocket. What's with you and nuts?" He soaked a piece of waffle in a huge puddle of Québec maple syrup.

*So much sugar. Gross.*

"Nuts are healthy for you." I pointed to his plate. "Do you really need so much?"

He held up the confection, with syrup dripping. "But of course." Then he shoved it into his mouth.

His gorgeous sexy mouth.

Which I totally shouldn't have been noticing.

But did.

Peter hadn't said my new boss was gay. And why would he, even if he knew?

Me? Well, I sort of wore it. In my clothes, mostly. Although I'd yet to show him my rainbow bow tie and my suspenders. I was saving those for a special occasion. I nibbled a piece of burger, then swallowed. "Okay, so what do you do in your spare time? Got a wife? Girlfriend?" I bit the bullet. "A boyfriend? Husband?"

He arched an eyebrow at me. "Not subtle at all, Ethan."

I shrugged. "So, I'm nosy. Peter said you'd need help with everything, and I guess I'm curious if I'm catering to just you or you and another person. And, like, I totally don't mind helping out. I'm great with kids—but I don't think you have kids. And how about pets? Oh, do you have a dog waiting for you at home? Of course you don't—you never would've brought me here if you had a dog waiting at home. And, like, do you often come out this far? Like do you go even farther? Like Chilliwack? Or Hope? Oh, do you go up to Whistler? Lots of rich people live in Whistler. I mean, you don't just help rich people, I assume. You said you didn't. Didn't you? But, like, rich people need help a lot, apparently, if the last twenty-four hours in your life are any indication." I leaned in. "Peter Erickson, Ed Markham, and some rich business tycoon with a playroom." I winked.

He blinked. "You knew?"

I rolled my eyes. "I wasn't born yesterday. I do know about BDSM. That couple? They seem so...normal..."

"Because they *are* normal. People who engage in BDSM are, for the most part, quite normal."

"You know a lot of them?" I bounced in my seat. "Can I meet more of them? Oh, do you know who else you're helping this week, or do you just see who texts you next? Because I have to admit that's a pretty cool way to live. On the edge, right? Never sure where the next assignment will be. Never knowing who you'll see that day. That's...awesome."

He blinked again. "Do you happen to have an off switch?"

"Ha! Good one." I scooped up my massive burger, eyed it, met Kingston's gaze, then tried to figure out the best way to bite the mammoth thing without spilling half of it down my shirt. "So, husband, wife, or something in between?" I bit.

He let out a sigh. "I trust you won't talk while you eat—"

I nodded. Tempted, but would restrain myself.

"No husband, wife, boyfriend, or girlfriend. And before you ask, no BDSM either." He glanced around, but we were surrounded by empty booths.

The closest filled one to us held a man, a woman, and two girls who appeared to be about four years old. Everyone was laughing and smiling, and the scene reminded me of when Gran used to take me out to White Spot on Pirate Day. I'd had the same level of excitement as the girls I observed.

Kingston, clearly having realized we were quite alone, held my gaze. "You're nosy. I have to say I don't appreciate that. Peter recommended you, though."

"Peter's paying me." I winced. "I was *not* supposed to say that."

He arched that damn eyebrow at me again. "Well, that answers the question of how much I'm paying you and whether I need to add you to my nonexistent payroll account."

"I wasn't supposed to tell you. I mean, if you tried to pay me, Peter said to refuse." I scratched my nose. "He also said, uh, to have you call him if that didn't work."

Kingston rolled his eyes. "You are a challenge."

"Well, that's the point, isn't it? You need someone who will stand up to you and force you to do what you're told." I pointed to his ankle. "You weren't even going to ask to elevate it, even though you're supposed to."

He jutted his chin out.

"Right. So you're planning to do everything yourself while you should be focused on taking care of that ankle until you feel better. It feels better. Whatever. Anyway, let's be clear. Peter's paying me. Does he feel guilty about what happened? Of course he does. Was it a freak accident? Of course it was. Now, to make him feel better, you're going to accept the help and be gracious."

"But—"

I held up my hand.

He blew out a breath.

I did a little victory dance in my head. "You've got me for six weeks. So make use of me. Take up a hobby while I take care of you. Watch all those streaming shows and movies you planned to watch but never had the time. Keep the ankle elevated while I do everything you need. Just be a good boy."

Another arch of the eyebrow.

I waved my hand. "You know what I mean."

"No." He eyed his food. "I'm not good at accepting help. I've been doing everything on my own for all of my adult life. My parents were independent, and they raised me to be self-sufficient. I have enough money in the bank to pay you—"

I started to speak.

This time, he waved his hand. "But I understand about both guilt *and* graciousness. Peter feels guilt. I can assuage that guilt by being gracious. Okay, so that's pretty straightforward. You, however, are a variable I simply hadn't anticipated." He shoved a forkful of waffle into his mouth.

*His first mistake.*

"Right. Perfect. So we're in agreement. Alignment. A meeting of the minds."

He nodded, all while chewing.

"So I'm assuming in that nice house of yours that you have a spare bedroom."

His eyes widened, but he couldn't speak. Not while he had food in his mouth.

"I'm going to move in. I think I have an out-of-town gig in a few weeks, but I can bow out if you're not self-sufficient and mobile by then. But no rushing it just to get rid of me. The doctor said six weeks. So you're going to take six weeks. Some sprains are worse than breaks—like yours is. You're going to do everything I tell you to do. And yes, Peter explained, in great detail, everything the doctor told you."

Kingston waved his fork then swallowed.

"Yeah, you're probably going to regret letting him stay with you during that part of the appointment. But Peter told me, I wrote it down, and now we're about to be best friends." I winked. Then bit into the best burger I'd ever tasted.

"Do I get a say in this?"

I held a hand before my mouth. "Do you want to upset one of the biggest movie stars on the planet?"

Again, Kingston blinked. Almost like he simply hadn't framed the problem that way before. And I could see why. Kingston didn't judge his clients by how much money they did or didn't have—he just did his job.

I liked that about him.

That also meant, however, that he hadn't considered the ramifications of not accepting my help. So I'd enlighten him. "If you don't allow me to help, then Peter plans to get someone to do the cleaning and cooking, someone to take care of the outside maintenance and leaf raking, and someone to do snow removal, should that be an issue." I scrunched my nose. "And anyone else who might be needed. So you can accept just one person disrupting your routine or you can deal with multiple people. And you still need to get around—unless you plan to take six weeks off work. He'd prefer that, but suspected you wouldn't be that smart."

He frowned. But didn't try to speak.

"Right. So you can take taxis all over town. Or Peter can hire you a driver who just sits around all day waiting to help you. Will that person be as discreet as me? I've got secrets, Kingston. I can keep yours as well." I took another bite of burger.

He pursed his lips. "You plan to do all that?"

Again, I held my hand in front of my mouth. "Do you do all those things yourself?"

He appeared to consider.

I swallowed. "Right. And you work full-time. So you focus on work, and I'll keep your house running. Sounds like a pretty good deal to me."

"I'm going to regret this. Something tells me that I'm really going to regret this."

An hour later, after I'd consumed another cup of coffee and he'd polished off a chocolate lava cake, I pointed the van toward Vancouver, and we were off. I chatted about my childhood, the mild autumn we'd had, as well as the Canucks' chance of winning the Stanley Cup this year.

Spoiler alert—less than zero.

Kingston stared moodily out his side window. At least he wasn't a side-seat driver who second-guessed everything I did.

When I mentioned that, somewhere in my monologue, he pointed out he'd accepted his fate.

I considered asking what that meant. But then decided I probably didn't want to know.

We stopped at my place so I could grab my packed suitcase—I hadn't wanted to carry it on the bus this morning—then we were on our way. Dusk had already fallen when I pulled into his driveway. I activated the remote for the garage door, then drove in. I cut the engine, then hit the button for the door to close. "I love technology. It isn't always my friend, but I do love it."

He grunted.

"Well, I doubt the original house came with the remote."

"Given the house is one hundred years old? That's a safe bet." He unbuckled his seatbelt.

I did the same and hurried over to his side. I handed him the crutches, and he grunted.

In what I assumed was gratitude. Hard to tell with him.

I inserted the plug into the van so it could recharge. "Okay, does anything from the van need to come inside?"

He shook his head.

"Does anything from inside have to come out? Are you going to replace the deadbolt with inventory you have, or do we need to stop by a store to buy another one tomorrow?"

He blinked.

I glared back. "Just because I don't have a regular job doesn't mean I don't understand the principles of just-in-time inventory management and supply-chain logistics."

Again with the blinking.

*God, does he think I'm incapable of doing anything? Of comprehending how business might operate? Huh. Possibly not. Should I tell him about my education? Nope, better not.* Didn't want to blow his mind all at once.

He gestured to the door with his chin. "Take off your shoes and socks before you enter the house. You're going to wash your feet and dry them first before you go any farther than the mudroom."

Now came my turn to blink. "Come again?"

"You heard me. No one wears socks or shoes in my house. Feet must be clean. And if you're truly here to help, you should know I sweep the floors once a day and wash them every third day."

I squinted. "But you don't allow shoes in the house? How can the floors get that dirty? Oh, do you have a cat and she sheds? Gran used to have this Himalayan cat. Lovely lap cat. Lazy as all get-out. She shedded something fierce. Gran had me vacuuming all the time. Which I didn't mind, because I liked Whiskers. Was sad when she passed. Wasn't entirely unhappy when Gran didn't replace her."

"I don't have a cat." He moved toward the door. "Are we clear about the rules?"

"Uh, sure." I pointed to his feet. "You realize, if we follow your rules, that I'm going to have to wash your feet as well."

He cocked his head as if in contemplation. As if this hadn't actually occurred to him. "Well... I'll make an exception for myself."

"And how are you going to shower? Or a bath might be better. Except how are you going to get out of the tub? I guess you're going to need my help, and—"

"Let's cross that bridge when we come to it."

"Right. You must be tired. Are you in pain? Oh, I should've been asking that all along. Do you need painkillers? Like anti-inflammatories or something? Because your ankle looks swollen again. Should I be worried? Like, if the cast is on too tight then you might lose circulation, and you might develop a clot or necrosis or something like that and they'd have to amputate your leg to save your life, and that sounds pretty horrific, but, like, if that's the only way to—"

"Ethan." Cold, quiet, and clearly calculated.

"Uh, yeah?"

"You're going to take your shoes off, and you're going to help me take mine off. We're going to go inside. You're going to wash and dry your feet. Then I'm going to sit on the sofa, and you're not going to talk until after the national news is finished. Do you think you can do that?

*Uh, crap.*

*I talk too much.*

*I always talk too much.*

"Sure. But, first, do you need me to go grocery shopping, or start laundry, or...you said sweep the floors, right? Can you at least point me to where the broom is? Then I'll be quiet. I mean, unless I think it's an emergency. Like if the smoke detector goes off, then I'm going to stay something—"

"If the smoke detector goes off, then I'll hear it as well. I am perfectly capable of hearing everything. Including your incessant blathering."

*Don't be hurt. He's in pain. He's grumpy. He doesn't intend to be mean to me. He's just...insensitive sometimes.* Not with clients, though. Just with me.

"I'm sorry, I didn't mean—"

"No, that's okay." I held up my hand. "I am a little much. Let me grab my suitcase so that I don't have to come back for it. Then, yeah, I'll help you take your shoes and socks off, and everything will be okay.

*Because it has to be.*

# Chapter Five

Kingston

*I'm an asshole.*
*No news here...just move along.*
*I've hurt his feelings.*

That stuck in my craw.

I hadn't meant to hurt his feelings. The kid felt impenetrable. Like things would just bounce right off him. Apparently, I'd been wrong.

He washed his feet, dried them with a fresh towel, then bent.

"What are you doing?"

"Washing your feet." He gazed up at me. "You said you don't allow dirty feet in your house. I'm assuming you meant yours as well. Or did you mean—"

"No, you're right." I sighed. "I'm not asking you to wash my feet. That's too much to ask. So's the rest of it, but you seem hellbent on this—"

"I am."

"—so I figure capitulating is easier than fighting."

"It is."

"But I draw the line at foot washing."

"Uh, okay." He rose. "Are you hungry? Because I think you ate a lot of food, but you're a big guy, and—"

"I'm sated, thank you." Better to head him off at the pass before he started one of his rambling monologues. They irritated. Well, I could find one distinct advantage.

They rarely required a response from me.

Something about just being able to sit without anything expected of me was appreciated.

He just needed to learn how to read a room.

*You're a tough nut to crack. You know that.*

Yeah, I did.

With difficulty, I maneuvered to the powder room.

I closed the door with a gaping Ethan on the other side.

*Jesus, did he think I needed him to hold my pecker while I peed?*

I wouldn't put it past him.

"I'm here in case, you know, you fall or something..."

Only then did I realize the precariousness of trying to piss without two solid legs to stand on.

I managed.

Barely.

*Six fucking weeks of this? I'm up shit creek without a paddle.*

Yet people managed. Perhaps I needed to research this on the internet. Because I'd never had to contemplate anything like this.

I balanced myself on one leg so I could wash my hands.

Forty years of being prodigiously careful. Well, perhaps before the age of two I might've been reckless—but from an early age I'd understood the concept of risk and had avoided it assiduously. I hadn't wanted to worry my parents unnecessarily. Wanted them to live long stress-free lives.

Yet I'd lost them both when they'd been in their seventies.

That felt too young.

"Uh, Kingston..."

*How long have I been standing here? Wait, has he been listening at the door?* He would've been able to hear the toilet flush...so had he been calculating exactly how long everything should take.? Oh God, I had to get him off that track. I did things at my own pace. My own speed. Always had and always would. Meticulousness was critical in my vocation. Shortcuts and sloppy work were recipes for disasters.

After staring at the mirror for a long moment—and grimacing at the stubble, I exited the bathroom.

Ethan stood there.

"As you can see, I didn't fall in."

He grinned. "I know that. I didn't hear a splash."

I refrained from pointing out how weird that statement sounded. "I was thinking about watching the news. Would you like to join me?"

"Uh, sure." He moved aside.

I managed to get myself onto the couch with relatively little trouble. And I let out a big sigh.

"Do your pits hurt? Mine always hurt—especially the very first day because my underarms weren't used to...what?"

"Precisely how often have you required crutches in your life?" I snagged the remote off the side table, but waited for his response.

"We need to elevate your leg. And how are your feet not cold?"

I blinked. I seemed to be doing that a lot because he said the oddest things. "Why would my feet be cold?"

"Because, I don't know, it's nearly winter? You should've been wearing a jacket today, but I didn't have time to suggest it, and I guess you don't spend much time outside unless you're working on a front-door lock. Oh, or a car lock. Do you do car locks? That would be super interesting. To hear all the ways people lose their keys. Can you tell me the most creative excuse you've had? Or is there something like locksmith/client privilege?"

I sighed. "There is nothing like locksmith/client privilege. There's discretion. Something, as I've made clear, that I'm known for. The most creative is the gentleman who threw his keys into the dumpster when he was throwing out the trash. He offered me a considerable sum of money to climb into the dumpster to retrieve them."

Ethan's eyes widened comically. "And did you?"

"For that sum of money? Yes, yes I did. He was offering me ten times what I would have made re-keying his condo lock. Also, he had keys for his safe deposit box and his drawer at the office." I considered. "Well, I would've done decently if he'd hired me to re-key everything but, frankly, the dumpster was easily dealt with. Fortunately, all the garbage was in sealed bags. I needed less than ten minutes to retrieve them."

"I'm sorry..." He cleared his throat. "You crawled into a dumpster?"

"Well, the remote for his car was also there, so that would've meant more expense for him and—"

"You wash your feet when you come into your house, but you'll scavenge dumpsters?" He scratched his scalp under the mop of red hair. "I don't get it."

"The two are completely unrelated."

He opened his mouth. Then snapped it shut. Then opened it again...only to clearly stall out.

I glanced at the wall clock.

Two minutes to six.

Assuming the conversation had terminated, I pressed the power button on the remote control.

My home channel was the twenty-four-hour news station, so I didn't even need to change the channel. I shifted, trying to find a comfortable position.

Ethan gently moved the coffee table so I could rest my foot on it.

Something I couldn't have done for myself

Wouldn't have done.

Everything had its place, and moving something was completely illogical. Except the pain eased instantly when I elevated the foot.

"I'll get you cold packs for your pits. Eight." Then he was gone.

*Eight?*

*Oh, times he's needed...holy hell.*

I couldn't fathom injuring lower limbs that frequently. And he was still just a kid.

*Not a kid. Twenty-four is most definitely not a kid. Twenty-four is very legal.*

The music for the national newscast began, and I straightened. As if somehow this was going to be the night something important happened in the world. Something to change the shitshow we were living through.

*Dream on. Second verse, same as the first.*

Real political sea change was required, and I couldn't see that happening. We needed things to change. But that felt impossible.

In my little bubble, though, things were okay. People would always need locksmiths. The government in British Columbia tended to sway left, but even the occasional knock to the right was never too sharp. At the national level, things were far less stable. To our north was Russia. To our south was the States.

Sometimes I felt we were being squeezed on all sides.

The lead story was about some political infighting in Ottawa.

Great. Politics.

Second story mentioned something going on in the States.

Great. More politics.

The third story was on a freak snowstorm that shut down the TransCanada Highway in Saskatchewan after an eleven-vehicle pileup that killed two people.

Wonderful.

I nearly turned off the broadcast.

Except Ethan clomped down the stairs, clearly having taken his suitcase to the spare bedroom, and perhaps even settled in.

"Did I miss anything?" He tucked his feet under him as he plopped onto the couch.

"Nothing of any consequence. It's all...depressing."

"Well, yeah. All news is depressing. Oh, hey, fast-forward through the commercial."

"Huh?"

He pointed to the television. "You don't need to see a commercial about upset-stomach medication. I mean, unless you have an upset—"

"I do not." But I might need headache medication if you keep this up. "I cannot fast-forward through the commercial. I'm watching a live broadcast."

He gaped. "You watch *live* television? Oh God, I didn't know people did that anymore. I watch everything on recording so I can fast-forward through the commercials. I mean, why watch those pesky things if you don't have to?

I nearly responded with a knee-jerk reaction. I wanted to watch the news at six o'clock. That meant, generally, sitting at the television at this time. I had it set to record in case I was out on an emergency call, but most nights, I was right here.

*But you could wait twenty or thirty minutes and then start recording. You wouldn't be more than a few minutes behind the news, and you could skip the advertisements...*

In forty years, this had never occurred to me. Unless I was away from the television, I watched the news at six. Then I did my dishes, tidied the house, swept and/or mopped the floor, and got changed into my pajamas between seven and seven-thirty. Then I watched *Jeopardy* followed by an hour of reading in my bedroom before bed.

Same routine for so long that I couldn't fathom anything else. I might stay up late on the weekends to watch a movie...but almost never. "I'll take your recommendation into consideration for another evening. But for tonight—"

The news broadcast recommenced.

So did Ethan. He chatted away even as I tried to focus on the television. News was of the utmost importance, and I wanted to tell him to stop, but I also didn't want to hurt his feelings again.

"Hey, would you mind running to the store for some milk?"

He stopped. "Of course not. Is there anything else you need?"

"No, thank you." I pulled my wallet out of my back pocket and, to my relief, he took the cash I offered.

"Back in a flash." He snagged the keys and was gone.

The closest grocery store was a fair distance, so I'd bought myself some time. I settled back to enjoy the rest of the broadcast in peace, barely stirring up anger when the political panel argued about the latest stupid thing someone here in Canada had done and although, yeah, the politician was clearly a dumbass, this felt...so small. Like so many bigger things were happening in the world.

"And I'm back. Washing my feet!" Ethan's voice carried from the mudroom.

Moments later, the sound of heavy grocery bags clunking on the counter reached me.

"I also bought bread, oranges, pineapples, an avocado, eggs, bell peppers, and peanuts."

*Of course he did.*

"I just saw this stuff and thought you'd like it. Oh, and I didn't forget the milk. I'll just put it away and...hey!"

*Shit.*

"Did you know you already have a four-liter jug in here? And that it's almost full?"

The final segment of the news was some feel-good story that felt almost too happy, so I shut the show off.

Ethan appeared in the doorway. "Did you send me to the store to get me out of your hair for twenty minutes?"

"You talk too much." I placed the remote on the side table. "And it worked."

I expected him to look crestfallen at my words, but he merely grinned. "That's okay, I'm going to make you a salad for dinner. After those waffles, you don't need anything heavy."

"I don't eat salad." Blech. Just...blech.

His jaw dropped open. "No salad? Lettuce, tomatoes, chopped pepper, and cucumbers? With a touch of peanut dressing? How can you not love salad?"

"Did you buy any berries?" I wasn't into fruits and vegetables but could gorge on blueberries. Too late in the season, but still...

"No berries. You should've said something." He stomped off.

Moments later, the sound of groceries being put way made its way to me—the swish of produce bags and the crinkling paper of... Huh.

I never bought vegetables and fruits—aside from berries—so I had no concept of what containers they might come in.

After a moment, the slamming of the microwave door ricocheted through the main floor of my house. Although it had the traditional multi-room layout, as opposed to the open concept favored by many homebuilders today, noise carried exceedingly well.

And since I never had company—had never had a partner or even a roommate—none of that mattered.

Until now.

*Six weeks. It's just six weeks.*

My phone rang, offering me a reprieve. I didn't even check the number. "Hello?"

"Kingston? It's Peter Erickson."

*Like I know many other Peters...* "Hello. How are you?"

"I was about to ask you the same question. How's the ankle?"

"Getting better." I eyed the damn thing—a bit less swollen since I'd propped it up.

"I'm not certain whether to believe that, but we'll put that aside for the moment."

Despite myself, I smiled at his dry tone. He was right, of course. Very few sprained ankles resolved in a day.

"How is Ethan working out? He's a great guy, and I hope he's making himself useful."

Said guy flounced into the room, and his eyes widened as he realized I was on the phone. He plopped a bowl of something onto the side table and almost scurried out of the room. Truly...I had no other word for it.

I glanced into the bowl.

Vanilla ice cream with heated blueberries.

I blinked. Several times.

# UNLOCKED AND UNLOST 53

"Kingston? Are you there?"

"Sorry, Peter." I cleared my throat. "He's a great guy. You're right. I probably could've coped on my own. People do."

"But not people with your job. I mean, I would've given you income commensurate with your lost—"

"I have to keep working."

"Hence my sending Ethan. And this is good for him as well."

"How so?" *That sounded casual...right? Yeah, tell yourself that.*

"Well..." Peter's wince came through the phone. "His gran says he needs stability. That he hasn't really had that, even with his business diploma."

"He was able to sit still long enough to get a business diploma?"

This time, Peter chuckled. "I know, right? But he's whip-smart. Just...unfocused."

After a moment, Peter's previous comment struck me. "You spoke to Ethan's grandmother?" I didn't bother to keep the surprise from my voice.

He laughed yet again. "She made baklava for Thomas and me as well as a sweater for Skylar and a scarf for Samuel."

Peter and Thomas's children.

"How long was Ethan working for you?" Disbelief laced my voice.

"Oh, on and off for a little while. I think he was embarrassed by the gifts, but didn't want to disappoint his grandmother by not giving them. Now, did she have them lying around or did she make them especially for my kids? Does that matter? They're exceptionally well made and incredibly generous gifts. She even made Skylar's sweater in a hunter green so Samuel will be able to wear it when she grows out of it and he's big enough. And I have to say—she's always been petite, and he's going to be a big, strapping boy. We're taking bets on how old they'll be when he outgrows her. Which will displease her to no end."

"She likes being an older sister?" I was still digesting the fact Ethan's grandmother made a sweater and scarf for two children she'd never met. Children whose parents were amongst the wealthiest in the city. Well, nearer the top than I ever would be. Vancouver had a lot of *very* wealthy people.

Peter sighed. "She loves it. She dotes on him. He's had health issues, so she knows she has to be gentle with him. Her soul's in the right place. That tricycle maneuver—"

"Already forgotten. Ethan's great." Because without Skylar, I wouldn't have a redheaded whirling dervish in my life and somehow, despite everything, I would've been poorer for that. Although...longest nine hours of my life.

"Well, that's great. I'm suspect he's told you I'm paying his salary..."

"He's very bad at keeping secrets." I rolled my eyes.

"Well, he'll keep the secrets of your clients."

"So he says."

"He will. He might come across as..."

"Flaky?"

"Well, I wouldn't have put it quite so bluntly, but...sure. But he takes things seriously when he has to. He apologized for telling his grandmother about us, and I'm quite certain he hasn't told anyone else that he works for us from time to time."

"Thank you for paying him, but it's unnecessary."

"No, it's really necessary. I've added him to my payroll, so the various premiums—including unemployment insurance, pension, worker's compensation, and healthcare are taken care of as well."

The first three were mandatory government programs, and although Canada had free healthcare, secondary services like prescriptions, and most paramedical professionals, weren't covered either. "You're too generous, Peter."

"Do I need to share how much the studio's going to pay me for the action film I'm making with Cole Hamilton next year? Or point out I saved my earnings for nearly twenty years before I met Thomas, and he's frugal as heck, so even now I don't spend all that much?"

"I didn't realize you and Cole were reuniting on the big screen." *Right, because* that's *the most important part of this conversation.*

"What can I say? He and I make a little movie about two gay men falling in love, and then we each come out as gay and bisexual, and the internet explodes. Now, so many fans want to see us do another movie. The studio's keen. Especially given I'm not getting any younger. You have no idea the workouts I'm having to endure just so I can survive."

I smiled as I envisioned Peter all sweaty. For a guy in his mid-forties, he looked damn good. Sexy. With a sweet personality to boot. "Well, I'll buy a ticket for that."

"I'll get you a ticket to the première . You and Ethan."

*What?*

"Oh, Thomas is waving. Samuel's bedtime. And Skylar soon after that. Let me know if you need anything, okay?"

Still stunned by his earlier comment, I managed a meek, "Yeah, sure."

"Great." He disconnected.

I put the phone on the side table, grabbed my melting ice cream and contemplated the clusterfuck of my life.

# Chapter Six

Ethan

Kingston didn't normally work weekends if he could help it, so we just hung around his nice house. I tried to stay out of his way while I cleaned, but he kept gritting his teeth and saying the job I was doing was *fine*.

Yeah, I'd heard that word enough from my father growing up.

My other issue—and this was a big one—was Kingston's pantry.

I'd never seen so much junk food in my life. Pasta and plain tomato sauce—not even the veggie-added variety. Kraft Dinner—which was my favorite comfort food…maybe *once or twice* a month. Potato chips, crackers, waffles from a box, frozen French fries, cookies, cake mixes, pie crust mix…just junky carbs everywhere I looked. I enjoyed the very occasional treat, but I didn't eat frozen pizza every night of the week. Unless he stocked up when they were on sale. Clearly that's what he did. Well, and the sneak peek I took in his recycling bin. Unless he never took it out—which I doubted very much—he ate this damn crap all the time.

I was heartened to see eggs until I had to acknowledge he probably used them for baking crap. Heck, he bought sugar by the four-pound bag. Even Gran stuck to one pound at a time. I might've been somewhat relieved he cooked...except only bleached flour for as far as the eye could see. Sheesh, would oats or whole wheat flour really be so terrible?

Wanting not to create a stir, though, I held my tongue.

And decided I was going to expand his palate while I was here.

Friday night, I presented eggplant parmigiana with Caesar salad and a fresh-fruit platter featuring berries, cherries, and pineapple slices.

He grunted his way through the eggplant, ignored the salad, bypassed the pineapple, and devoured the berries without even sharing.

I pursed my lips, but held my tongue.

Saturday morning, I made a western omelet with roasted peppers and a side of handmade baked hash browns.

He wrinkled his nose at the omelet and doused the hash browns in ketchup, but he ate the peppers without making a face, so I took that as a win.

Saturday for lunch, I handmade a whole-wheat pizza with ham, green peppers, mushroom, and pineapple.

He picked off the peppers and pineapple, but ate the mushrooms and didn't say anything about the whole wheat.

Score me.

He glanced around the kitchen. "Did you have to use *every* dish in the place?"

"I said I'd clean it up. Do you want a carrot?"

"I want a cookie."

"Too bad. I threw them all out."

His jaw dropped. "You what?" He might've sputtered that.

I pursed my lips. "One cookie."

"I knew you didn't throw them out." He narrowed his eyes at me.

"One cookie," I repeated. "If you eat a piece of pineapple."

He squinted.

"One piece, and you get that maple-flavored, sugar-filled, diabetes-waiting-to-happen cookie."

"Hey!"

"Which part of that was inaccurate?" I pursed my lips right back. "How do you look so good when you eat such crap?" *Oops. Didn't mean to point out how attractive I find him. Because, damn, he's got a nice body.* He wore boxers to bed and, apparently, wasn't worried about me seeing him in them.

Oh, and shirtless. His muscular chest was lightly dusted with dark hair down to his happy trail and under the boxers.

"Crap? I don't eat crap. Crap is vegetables and spinach pasta and—" He gestured to his plate. "—pineapple."

"Have you ever tried pineapple?" *And thank you for focusing on that and not that I think you're sexier than sex-on-a-stick Peter Erickson...*

"Well...no..."

"Okay, so one piece of pineapple gets you one cookie. Fair trade."

"I can just grab the entire bag—"

"That assumes you know where to look." *In my room at the top of the closet, but I figure you're not going to go looking there, and if you do, then we have much bigger problems than violating my privacy.* Sugar addiction was a thing.

I'd searched it on the internet.

"You've got to be kidding me." Still, he speared a piece of pineapple and ate it.

At first, he wrinkled his nose as he chewed. Then, slowly, his nose returned to normal.

Well, I'd always found it a little snubbed...in a cute way. He had a round face—but not fat. Just...adorable. His dark hair was close-cropped and his lips appeared kissable.

*Don't stare.*

He met my gaze with those too-knowing bright-gray eyes.

Heat crept from my chest, up my neck, and onto my cheeks. From experience, I'd be nearly bright red in mere moments.

I pushed away from the table.

"Hey, where's my cookie?"

"I'll bring it to you once you're settled back onto the couch with your feet—"

His phone buzzed. He grabbed it, swiped, and arched an eyebrow. "Well, this should be interesting." He gestured with his chin. "You up for a drive to Coquitlam?"

"Of course." I hustled to put all the leftovers in the fridge and as many dishes into the dishwasher as I could.

I was trying to figure out how to turn it off when he said, "Don't. I never leave it running when I'm not home. We'll turn it on when we get home."

"Yeah, okay. You need a coat?"

The weather had turned again, bringing an arctic chill that wasn't common in November.

"Sure. The young woman is waiting at a neighbor's house until we get there."

I grabbed his coat and helped him into it. Then I managed to get us into socks and shoes. Finally, we left the house. He set the alarm, and we got into the van. Within just a couple of minutes, we were on the way.

"Where in Coquitlam? Does it make sense to take the Number 1 or the Barnet Highway?" I turned right onto Hastings Street and headed away from downtown Vancouver. Regardless of our journey, we were going to drive right through my neighborhood. That prospect excited me. Obviously we wouldn't be stopping, but I always got a kick out of passing through my stomping grounds.

"The GPS says there's an accident near Deer Lake Parkway on the Number 1, so we might as well use the Barnet. Prettier drive."

I arched an eyebrow but kept my eyes on the road. I never would've figured him for someone who enjoyed a *pretty* drive. He just seemed...practical. That said, I'd spotted a few garden gnomes, and a stork stuck in his garden, so he did enjoy aesthetically pleasant things as well as the mundane.

The garden needed work before the first frost came, so I planned to tackle that tomorrow. If he wanted to supervise, I could bundle him up with blankets and put him in a chaise lounge. The sun was supposed to be out, so he'd need sunglasses and a hat to complement the puffy coat and piles of comforters.

*Do you want him watching you? Criticizing you and sarcastically commenting?*

Good point.

*Yeah, but then he could watch my ass.*

True.

He hadn't *actually* come out as gay, but all the signs were there. Including him checking me out several times in an *I'm checking you out* kind of way. Straight guys sometimes did that—I was sort of unique—but the glances from Kingston? More predatory.

Which totally turned me on.

And I didn't hide my sexuality. Today's outfit was a rainbow bow tie, matching suspenders, a pale-pink dress shirt, and khaki pants. Not that a straight guy couldn't pull off the look...but probably not as well as I did.

I put my foot to the floor to make it through the intersection before a light turned red.

"Hey." Kingston hung onto the door.

"No one was turning left." I shrugged. "No one waiting to turn right in the northbound traffic. So, we were fine."

"So you say."

I passed a slower-moving car in the left-hand lane. I didn't give the guy a piece of my mind. Well, out loud anyway. In my head I strenuously suggested he stick to the slow lane and keep out of the way of people who were—

*Crap.*

Sixteen klicks over the limit.

I eased off the gas.

Soon enough, though, we were headed into the Burrard Inlet. Beautiful, tall trees soared to our right while the water lapped gently on the shore to our left. Traffic was light and, for just a moment, we were the only vehicle in sight.

The highway and our van felt out of place amongst the majesty.

Until I saw the fuel terminal. The end of the pipeline.

Reality hit hard. We were still a carbon-based society. Making progress, for certain, but not there yet.

Then we hit the town of Port Moody and civilization returned. I liked this quaint part of the trip and even followed the speed limit. As soon as I could, though, I picked up my speed again.

"She lives on the Westwood Plateau, so we'll need to take a right-hand turn up ahead." Kingston's voice broke the extended silence.

I glanced at the dashboard.

*Wow, you went an entire twenty-two minutes without saying something while being in another's presence.*

*Are you okay?*

I snickered to myself. Careful not to speak aloud. Let Kingston think I was snickering at him. "That's great."

Even as I said the words, mister sexy Aussie told me to turn.

And I followed his instructions all the way into a nice little neighborhood with single-family houses as far as the eye could see. Cities needed densification. Greater Vancouver was running out of room, and we needed to build up as much as possible. Coquitlam had some areas that were definitely clustering—mostly around transit hubs.

"You have arrived at your destination."

"Thank you." I pulled the van to the curb and parked in front of a two-story white-sided house. Much the same as the others except this one had a bright-yellow door. Something to differentiate it from the others.

"Did you just thank the GPS?"

I met Kingston's incredulous stare.

After a moment, I both shrugged and smiled. "I thank elevators when they announce my floors, ATMs that dispense my cash, and GPS devices that help me arrive safely. Hey, is that the lady?"

A woman with hair almost as dark as Kingston's emerged from the house next door and waved frantically.

"Safe bet."

I was out of the van and around with Kingston's crutches just in time. I always worried if I wasn't quick enough that he'd just put weight on the ankle—consequences be damned.

Her dark-gray eyes, also like Kingston's, flashed appreciation. "Hi! I'm so grateful you could make it. You had to come a long way, I know.

But Hallstein swore you're the best." She fluttered her hands. Then clearly caught herself as she frowned and lowered them.

I didn't ask who *Hallstein* was.

"He was correct to refer me. And we didn't mind making the drive. Very scenic." Kingston smiled.

Yes, smiled.

"Well, that's true. And he told me how you rescued him and Myles when they accidentally got stuck in that janitor's closet." She winked.

*Ah, that dude. So is Hallstein the head of security or the set decorator?* I made a mental note to ask later.

"Yes, well." Kingston cleared his throat. "I'm always happy to help. What seems to be the problem?"

"I'm so confused." She pointed to her front door. "I drove home and parked on the street because we're watching Kat's Jaguar while she's away. So it's in the garage. Gillian parks her SUV in there as well, and we're expecting guests for dinner, so I figured it would be easiest for me to leave the driveway clear for them."

I didn't even try to keep up.

"Okay." Kingston continued to hold her gaze.

"Right. So I made three trips of stuff from the car to the house, and when I went to unlock the front door, my keys were gone. Just…gone." She held her hands out as if that somehow emphasized her dilemma. And since her hands were empty, her flapping them around kind of did.

"It's okay." Kingston spoke in his softest and most soothing voice. "We'll get your house unlocked, and then we'll figure out what we'll do next."

"I had my work keys on that ring. That's at least two locks at the office. My car keys, the remote to my garage…" She winced. "I'm adding this up in my head, and it's not looking good. But, I mean, they have to be here somewhere, right? I had them when I drove up, and now I don't. I've looked *everywhere*." She said the word with great emphasis.

"No worries. Why don't I get to work?"

Taking that as my cue, I headed to the van. Within a couple of minutes, I had him set up on a folding chair in front of the front door.

"Oh, this is so great." The woman shivered. "Oh God, I haven't even introduced myself. I'm Tabitha." She waved her hand around yet again. "I should probably prove I live here or something."

"That would be appreciated." Kingston's gaze flicked from her to me and then back to her.

As she yanked her phone out of her back pocket, I backed away.

If Kingston needed me, he'd call. He had yet to, though. Sebastian had apparently helped him with the finicky lock while we'd been at his house.

Thinking of Sebastian reminded me of the lovely Tarah with her blue eyes, and that got me wandering down the sidewalk. The trees in his neighborhood weren't as old as mine, which had nothing to do with the color of Tarah's eyes, but the sky was darkening, and maybe it might rain? God knew, the temperature was dropping. Snow wasn't in the forecast, but meteorologists made mistakes, right?

Although probably not about us getting snow instead of rain.

My nose twitched.

*Dog.*

*Malamute or husky or beagle.*

All three carried distinctive smells, but this dog... Nope, I couldn't settle on one breed.

I followed the scent as it mixed with human.

A familiar human's.

Tabitha had been here.

And she'd interacted with the dog.

I smiled. Yeah, she seemed like someone who would stop to pet a dog. Friendly like that. Not just to Kingston because he was going to rescue her, but also just because she had that open and honest vibe.

Following the scent, I continued up the street.

Tabitha's scent disappeared while the dog's got stronger.

I wanted to put my nose to the ground, but didn't figure that would earn me any favors. Being a stranger was often a tough enough sell.

*Stop.*

I paid attention to my nose. I spun and headed up a driveway.

This house's front door was a plain beige—which matched the rest of the house. Well, some people didn't express their inner joy with bright colors.

I straightened my tie.

*Maybe zip your coat to cover it? What if they're not—*

The almightiest racket came from the front window.

I spun and my gaze connected with deep-brown eyes.

*Drat.*

Wrong call.

Chocolate lab.

She looked at me.

I held her gaze.

She stopped barking.

I stepped forward and rang the doorbell.

She started barking again.

"All right, Bluebell. I can hear the doorbell." An exasperated woman's voice rang out through the closed door.

The dog continued to bark.

*Bluebell?*

A rather harried-looking woman, with distinctive auburn curly hair, opened the door. She grabbed Bluebell by the collar just as the dog lunged for me.

I dropped to my haunches and held out my hand.

She eyed me, then sniffed.

More barking.

Yeah, if I sniffed myself, I'd bark as well.

I stood and smiled. "I'm so sorry to bother you."

The woman smiled tentatively. "Whatever you're selling—"

I shook my head. "Not selling anything. But I'm hoping you can help me. Your neighbor has lost her keys, and I was hoping you might have them."

She blinked. "I don't have anyone else's keys. I'd remember if..." She gazed down at Bluebell.

Who blinked up as if trying for innocent.

I twitched my nose.

She barked.

Her mom sighed. "Bluebell." To me, she held up a finger.

I nodded.

Bluebell and I continued to stare at each other. She knew my truth. Just like I knew, without a shadow of a doubt, that she was the key thief.

The nice lady reappeared a few moments later, wiping the keys down with a wet paper towel. "I'm so very sorry. I'm trying to get the slobber and dirt off. She hid them in her favorite spot in the backyard. I didn't even see her steal them." She eyed her dog.

Who glared at me as if she understood I was the one taking away her valued treasure.

"I'll let Tabitha know." I took the damp keys from her. "She'll be grateful."

"I don't know...oh, wait a moment. That lovely woman...with the wife..."

Tabitha being a lesbian—or bi—hadn't come up in casual conversation. I waved my hand. "Several streets over? Yes."

"She's always so nice when we walk by." The nice woman cocked her head. "How did you know Bluebell stole the keys? Or that she lived here?"

"A little birdie told me." I winked at Bluebell. "Gotta run."

"But—"

But nothing. I was out the door, down the driveway, and halfway down the street in a heartbeat. No way was I going to try to explain anything.

Bluebell knew.

Fortunately, she didn't have the linguistic prowess to explain me to her hapless human companion. Little demoness dog.

She *knew*.

I twitched my nose as I hustled. Then I turned onto Tabitha's street and moved even faster. I didn't want Kingston changing any locks since I'd rescued the keys and there was zero chance they'd been duplicated in the hour they'd been buried in Bluebell's backyard.

As I approached Tabitha's house, an SUV pulled into the driveway. The garage door opened, and the vehicle drove in.

The front door was on the other side of the house, so I moved gingerly that way.

"Gillian?" Tabitha came around the corner just as the other woman got out of her car.

"You didn't find your keys? Oh, honey." Gillian held out her arms in an obvious willingness to offer comfort.

I held up the keys, despite not wanting to interrupt what promised to be a touching moment. If I'd lost my keys, my dad wouldn't have been comforting me, that was for certain.

Tabitha stopped in her tracks. "Where in the hell did you find them?" She grasped Gillian's hand. "This is Ethan. He's Kingston's assistant."

"Kingston...?"

"The locksmith. He's just—" Her eyes widened. She snatched the keys from my hands and bolted around to the front door. "Kingston! Stop what you're doing!"

Gillian's eyes widened.

"Well, since we found her keys, and because no one copied them, you don't need new locks..." I shrugged.

"Okay." Gillian eyed me. "And where did you say you found the keys?"

"I didn't." My nose twitched.

She arched an eyebrow. "Try again. I know you're not part of a scam because you drove all the way from Vancouver, so that doesn't make sense."

"That I would randomly steal a woman's keys in Coquitlam? No, I'd say not."

"Tabitha spent an hour looking for them before she called Hallstein to warn him. She didn't even care about herself—or her situation. She only cared about the studio being compromised."

"Well, she doesn't need to worry. I can guarantee they weren't copied."

Her hand landed on her hip.

"Where did you say...?" Tabitha rounded the corner with Kingston awkwardly following her.

"It's a super long story, and Kingston needs to get off his feet, so if we're good to go..." I met his thunderous expression. *Oh shit. He's really pissed.*

"Sure—" Tabitha started to speak.

I started to move.

Gillian pressed a hand to my chest.

"Uh..."

"Just be honest." Kingston held my gaze. "No one is going to be upset. But if Tabitha isn't to make the same mistake again, she needs to know." No compassion, except perhaps for the harried woman who was, frankly, more distressed now than she had been when we'd arrived.

I swallowed. "Okay, but you have to promise not to say anything."

The three exchanged puzzled looks.

I took a breath. "I don't want the d-o-g in question to get in trouble."

"Bluebell!" Tabitha nearly shouted the name. "That little sneak." Her eyes flashed. "Okay, also super cute."

"Yeah," Gillian agreed. "Still." The woman eyed me. "What, was she sitting on her front lawn slobbering on them when you happened by?"

"In fact, that's exactly it. Her mom cleaned the keys and swore me to secrecy, but now you know. You'll be more careful around the thieving dog and, really, we don't ever need to discuss this again."

For a very, very, very long moment, we all stood still.

All three stared at me.

Tabitha waved her arms. "Okay. We're going to never discuss this again. But you're coming to dinner next Friday night so I can thank you properly."

"Oh, we couldn't—" Kingston tried.

She waved him off. "You don't want me telling Hallstein that after I dragged out all this way that you wouldn't accept our dinner invitation. Six sharp, please don't bring anything."

"Yes." Gillian linked arms with her wife. "You must come."

Kingston glared at me.

Right. Like the women blackmailing him was somehow *my* fault. I'd saved the situation, but was anyone giving me credit? Nope.

The drive home was *very* long.

# Chapter Seven

Kingston

I'd had enough.

Four days of infirmity.

Four days of crutches.

Four days of Ethan.

I was *thrilled* he'd found Tabitha's keys. I would've changed all the locks she needed me to. I even would've given her a bulk discount. But if someone could find their keys, then I was always thrilled for them. Better that, honestly. Even though replacing locks netted me more money.

The way Ethan found the keys, though, was highly suspicious. His explanation of just happening by and finding a dog on the front yard mouthing the keys was...implausible. First, there hadn't been any teeth marks. Whatever slobber there might've been was gone. And the promise he extracted from the women to never say anything? Made no sense. Unless he worried Bluebell might get in trouble. Well, damn dog did deserve to get in trouble. And the neighborhood needed to be warned.

Yet the women had promised, had paid me, and then manipulated me into accepting their dinner invitation next Friday night at their house.

With Ethan.

Obviously leaving him at home was impossible.

I eyed his closed bedroom as I quietly shut mine. So he'd think I was in there if he went to the bathroom.

Getting down the stairs as quietly as I could was a challenge, but I did my best. I had to get out of my fucking house. I loved the place, but I needed distance from Ethan.

That meant going for a run.

Silently—well, as silently as I could—I slipped out of the house and into the backyard.

The night air bit, but that invigorated me. I sat on a decorative bench I'd installed and removed my pajamas as well as the bandage. They'd be cold and damp to put back on, but I didn't care.

When I was naked, I shifted.

Muscles stretched. Bones cracked as they transformed.

Pain sliced through me.

But I didn't care.

In my animal form, human injuries didn't matter. I wouldn't be hobbled. I could run free.

As soon as I was fully shifted, I did one final stretch, and then I headed for my favorite oak tree. I scaled it easily and sat on a branch to get a lay of the land. This part of town had rats, squirrels, skunks, and racoons. The bears were across the bridge in North Vancouver and over in Burnaby and Coquitlam near the mountains. East Vancouver was flat with no discernible nature area. Parks, sure. But places for coyotes and bears to roam in peace? Nope.

I lumbered down to the fence and followed it to the front of my house.

After ensuring I was alone, I headed down the street toward MacLean Park. I loved the massive and abundant trees. I avoided the play areas because sometimes adults from the area hung around smoking cigarettes and pot. Loathing the smell—and not wanting to attract attention to myself—I avoided anywhere humans might congregate. Generally, though, the park was pretty quiet at night.

I chose a tree at random and scaled it easily.

*Oh, this is the best feeling in the world. I'm free.*

My human responsibilities often weighed on me, but when I was alone here, as a racoon, I could let all that go. I was lucky that I didn't have to forage for food. More importantly, I didn't have to go through garbage cans to find sustenance. I appreciated that. And I didn't judge my fellow creatures who had to. I just hoped they didn't make too much of a mess. We didn't exactly have a good reputation in the city.

My nose twitched.

*No. It can't be.*

The most marvelous scent enveloped me.

Heaven. I'd died and gone to heaven.

My father's words came back to me. *The scent of your fated mate will be your favorite scent in the world. You'll know instantly. And, if you're very lucky, they'll recognize it as well.*

I smelled vanilla sugar cookies.

*Did the scent come from one of the homes?*

*No, that would be ridiculous. The houses are far away from here, and everyone has their windows shut because it's nearly winter and, finally, it's the middle of the fucking night.*

Okay, so fated mate it was.

I descended the tree to get the lay of the land. It couldn't be a racoon—I knew everyone in the neighborhood. Male or female? In human form, I leaned gay, but I'd been with the occasional woman. My parents had been straight and very happy with each other. Whoever this creature was, I'd make it work.

Then I spotted the most gorgeous squirrel I'd ever seen. Their red fur gleamed in the glow from the streetlamp. Their bushy tail was larger and fluffier than I'd ever seen.

I sniffed again.

Male.

Well, that was fine. *I've found my fated mate! Here in my park!* Hopefully that meant they lived nearby.

He turned, his nose twitched, and he headed my way.

The closer we got, the more aroused I became. I wasn't inherently sexual. Sex was nice, but I didn't require it to function—either as a human or a racoon.

His tail swished as he moved toward me.

Mere inches apart, we sniffed.

His dark-brown eyes gleamed in obvious delight. He pressed a claw to my nose.

I leaned into the touch.

He came closer and pressed his nose to my forehead. Then he turned and ran.

*Game on.*

He wasn't running away from me.

No, we were playing a game of chase.

He easily scaled a maple tree.

I was hot on his heels.

# UNLOCKED AND UNLOST

When he leapt to the next tree, though, I lost my nerve. My inherently cautious nature as a human permeated my animal form as well. If I fell and broke something, I might not be able to shift back to human. Someone might come along and kill me.

I didn't like that idea.

The squirrel cocked his head.

Then jumped back.

He landed on the branch below me and scrambled back down the tree. He scurried over to some bushes and disappeared.

In a heartbeat, I followed.

When I caught up with him, in a well-protected area, we stopped to gaze at each other.

He cocked his head.

I nodded.

We shifted.

My focus was entirely on how quickly I could retake my human form and then how quickly we could come together. That primal urge to take, to mark, and to conquer was foremost in my mind. We didn't have condoms, but we didn't need to worry about diseases since our shifter genes protected us from both human and animal communicable illnesses. Lube would be nice, but we'd figure something out. Nothing mattered except—

*No. No. No. Oh God, no. Fucking hell.*

A very naked Ethan sat before me on the damp earth, his grin as wide as I'd ever seen it. For a squirrel shifter, he had very little body hair. The red fuzz covered his arms and legs, but not abundantly. His trimmed pubes helped emphasize his erect cock.

Mine, which had been equally interested, was quickly deflating.

He began to speak.

I held up my hand.

His dark-blue eyes gleamed. After a moment, he moved to his haunches, and his body vibrated. "Oh my God, Kingston. I love it! We didn't know, and now we know, and we're gonna be together, and we're gonna be happy, and oh my God, I am so happy, and I didn't think I would meet my mate, and I was so scared my mate was gonna be a girl, but this is just great, and...."

I took off and scurried home like the hounds of hell were on my heels.

And maybe they were.

I'd found my fated mate. And he happened to be the person I could least stand in the world. *Why, why, why?*

Since I didn't have a good answer, I shifted back to human. I held my clothes in my hands and somehow hobbled back to the house with the fucking crutches.

I locked all the doors and headed upstairs.

*Fuck my life.*

It took hours...but somewhere near dawn I finally slipped into a restless slumber.

I slept through my alarm.

Well, I probably turned it off and went right back to sleep.

At about ten, my bladder demanded attention. I managed to roll out of bed without banging my ankle. I held myself still.

Then remembered I'd locked Ethan out.

Which was probably a mean thing to do, but I couldn't have dealt with him last night. Hell, I wasn't certain I could deal with him ever again.

*Except you have a business, and you need a driver. He carries your equipment. He cooks healthy food for you.*

*Oh...I should look for the cookie stash.*

Piss first. A sponge bath while sitting on the toilet, fresh clothes, and then I could go on the hunt.

Thirty minutes later, though, the notion of searching for cookies was too much. For reasons I couldn't explain, I had a hankering for pineapple. And eggs.

*He's done this to you. Made you crave...healthy food.*

*Ugh.*

In the kitchen, I opened the fridge and tried to figure out if I could cook eggs while on crutches. In short? Hell fucking no.

I grabbed a couple of frozen waffles and put them in the toaster.

*Buzz.*

*Buzz.*

*Buzz*

*Right. Why ring the doorbell once when one can buzz it three times in a row?*

I was nearly to the door when Ethan pounded. "Let me in, Kingston! I had the best night ever. I told Gran about you, and she's happy for me, and she wants to meet you and all. Please unlock the door."

Another pound.

*Holy fuck.*

Yet I unlocked the door and opened it. "Get the hell in here." I ground out the words. "I don't think the entire neighborhood needs to know our business." I shut and relocked the door, all while balancing on my crutches.

He sniffed. "Cardboard waffles? Really?" He held up a bag from a sandwich store I knew. "They make the best breakfast sandwiches. Whole-wheat buns, egg yolks, avocado slices, and tomatoes. So healthy." He moved past me and toward the kitchen.

I followed as quickly as I could.

To find him dumping my waffles into the compost.

*They're compostable? Huh...*

He grabbed two plates and set about organizing the food.

I had to admit, it smelled...appealing.

"Sit. Sit. You need to elevate that ankle. I'll bet you haven't been doing that. See? You need me around."

Not wanting an argument, I sat.

He put our plates before us, organized two glasses of water, and plopped down as well.

Finally, he met my gaze. "What? Aren't you happy? How many jobs have we got today? You haven't had your coffee, have you? No problem. I'm going to make the coffee while you eat. I know, I know! Decaf for me. I don't need any more energy. You've told me six hundred times." He hopped up and headed for the coffee machine.

I was so discombobulated this morning that I hadn't even made coffee. That was always the first step. Everything else afterward was routine, but didn't matter half as much as the caffeine injection.

Then his words sank in. "I don't have any jobs today. It's Sunday. No emergency calls as of yet." I eyed my phone on the counter.

He grabbed it, put it by my hand, and continued to make my coffee. Eventually he put it in front of me, and I was surprised to discover I'd eaten most of the sandwich. The avocado hadn't even tasted slimy.

"So what is the plan for today?" He sat beside me and sipped his decaf.

"Honestly? I need a nap."

He cocked his head? "Nocturnal adventures too much? Oh, is your ankle making you tired? Your body needs to heal. It's giving you signals that you'd better not ignore. I'll keep your phone close to me so if something comes up, I'll let you know, but otherwise you can just rest. Gran says rest is so very important. And, like, shifting's hard work. I can't believe you're a shifter! Isn't that so cool? I mean, what are the odds? You don't think Peter and Thomas are shifters, do you? Or Ed and Thornton? No, probably not. I did wonder..." He scrunched his nose.

"What?" As much as I wanted him to just stay quiet, I was also intensely curious about what he was thinking.

"Do you..." He cocked his head. "Tabitha." He waved the thought away. "Never mind."

I sought, from the recesses of my mind, my memories of the woman with the long dark-brown hair and deep-gray eyes. So like my own. Even if she was a shifter, I couldn't fathom which she'd be.

Ethan, though? In retrospect, I could easily see how he'd end up being a squirrel shifter. Everything about him screamed showoff.

Well, if he'd turned out to be a peacock, that would've fit as well. Even today, he wore another rainbow tie, a pale-purple shirt, bright-blue suspenders, and—interestingly—boring khaki pants.

"You know how I recognized you?" He ducked his head for a moment, then caught my gaze. "Peanut brittle."

I held my coffee aloft, totally mesmerized by his bright-blue eyes. "Come again?"

"Peanut brittle. Of all my favorite foods—and I have many—peanut brittle is the best. I sniffed last night, smelled it, and knew." He nodded. "You?"

"Vanilla sugar cookies."

He burst out laughing. "Because of course you'd have cookies in there somewhere."

"I need to go upstairs. Would you mind...?" I gestured to the dirty dishes.

"Of course." He laid his hand on mine. "You take it easy. Maybe I'll make something special for lunch and I'll bring it up to you."

"That..." I resisted the urge to pull my hand back. This was *way* too much intimacy. "Thank you." I'd leave it at that.

I managed to hobble upstairs without too much effort. Leaving my phone behind was tougher than even the climb because I was never without it. I had chargers all over the house. One could never be too careful.

When I arrived at my bed, though, I just dropped. I propped the crutches against the nightstand and eyed my damn wrapped ankle.

Life felt full of possibilities—I'd met my fated mate.

Life felt full of obstacles—my fated mate drove me nuts on a regular basis.

*Nuts. Ha. Funny.* At least his obsession with peanuts made more sense.

I held my wrist to my nose and sniffed. Nope. No peanut brittle scent. Nothing that, I believed, would make me attractive. I was a soap-and-water kind of guy.

And Ethan, in his human form, didn't have a distinctive scent either.

*Admit it...you find him cute. Adorable. Sexy in a very twinky way.*

I pursed my lips. I didn't have a traditional *type*. When I dated, I sought intellectual equals. People—mostly men—who'd lived interesting lives.

Not twenty-four-year-old, barely-through-puberty motormouths who didn't know when to quit.

*Except you like all those things about him. He makes you feel young again.*

Again? When had I ever been young? I'd been born an old soul. Had been groomed, from a young age, to take over the family business. Had been singularly focused on being successful. Having a nice house, a comfortable living, and all the things a mate would find enticing.

Yet I'd never found a mate—fated or otherwise.

*Until now.*

Yeah, until—

"Why are you not lying down?" Ethan stood in the doorway holding a mug. "I made you some chamomile tea. To soothe you. You're frazzled."

Was I? I couldn't be certain of anything anymore. "That was kind. I didn't know I had chamomile tea."

"You didn't. I did a huge grocery shop this morning, and the delivery arrived. Didn't you hear it? Oh well, clearly you've got things on your mind." He put the mug on a coaster on the nightstand and then crawled onto the bed behind me.

To my shock.

He pressed his cheek against my shoulder blade. Then he wrapped his arms around my chest. "I know I'm a bit of a disappointment when it comes to a mate. But I'm going to be the best mate to you. Ever."

His words were said with such surety that I almost believed him.

Almost.

"I didn't say you disappointed me. I just don't know..." I drew in a deep breath and let it out slowly—willing my stress to recede. "What if we don't get along?"

"We're gonna be so happy together. You'll see. Here. Let me help you into bed." He shifted so he could guide me down, then he moved off the bed so he could brace my ankle as I lay back. "You didn't get much sleep last night. I can tell. I know you. You just sat and stressed all night."

"Well, not *all* night." I might've groused that—more because he already knew me so well and had my number as opposed to him making the comment at all.

"Come on, let me help you."

And so he did. He put a pillow under my ankle. He fluffed the pillow beneath my head. He pulled the throw blanket from the lounge chair and draped it over me.

All the while, he touched me. He caressed my toes—ostensibly to ensure I had proper circulation. He scratched my scalp as he straightened the creases in the pillow. He brushed his hand against my biceps as he adjusted the blanket.

Each touch had my nerve endings on high alert.

Those feelings from last night were back—claim, conquer, and mate. Make him mine.

I shifted, trying to hide my growing erection under the too-thin blanket.

"Oh." Ethan started at my crotch.

"It's nothing. I'm sorry. You're just..." I sighed. "You...well..." *Inarticulate much?*

"Well, you know I'd be happy to take care of that for you."

My eyes widened as I met his intense gaze.

"Oh?" *Right, because who needs words when you can just stare into those intense, deep pools of liquid?*

He ran his hand down my cheek.

And lower.

He caressed my chest.

And grasped the blanket, slowly lowering it.

"Ethan..."

"Say *no*. If you don't want this, just say no. You can always ask me to stop."

His earnestness spoke to me. I was all about consent and, without doubt, he'd halt if I asked.

*If.*

But I didn't want him to. "It's okay." I put my hands behind my head. "I'm sort of curious what you're going to do." Because, honestly, anything that involved my cock and just about any body part of his fascinated me.

He grinned. Then settled the blanket so it covered me from the knees to the tip of my toes. "So your feet don't get cold."

Given the heated look he was giving me, I doubted that was possible. Still, his consideration was appreciated. "Thank you."

"My pleasure." He moved to unbutton my dress shirt.

I couldn't help myself—if I wasn't wearing my uniform during the day then I was in a nice shirt. T-shirts were for evening relaxing.

As he bared skin, he pressed little open-mouthed kisses to my chest. When he had the thing completely unbuttoned, I lifted my hips so he could tug it out from my pants.

I expected him to continue his exploration downward, but he returned to my chest and, after giving me another of those heated stares, he took one of my nipples into his mouth.

It pebbled instantly, reacting to the warm wetness. To the suction. To the little nibbles. I'd never considered my nipples particularly sensitive, but with each swirl of his tongue, my cock hardened further. Part of me wanted him to continue this forever, and part of me wanted to beg he pay attention to things below my waist.

*Patience. He probably has more experience than you.*

Yeah, possibly.

Sure, probably.

He switched to my other nipple, and I shifted my hips, seeking some kind of friction. I'd never been this hard this quickly. Usually I had to work up to full arousal. With Ethan, though, it was zero to one hundred in mere moments.

"Patience." He chuckled.

"You have no idea what you're asking."

He winked. Then proceeded to lick his way down my sternum, to my navel, and lower still.

I grasped the blanket beneath me. *He's going to kill me.*

*Yeah, but what a way to go...*

True that.

He slipped my button open. Then he lowered my zipper.

*Finally.*

Another wicked grin as he slid his hand under the waistband of my briefs. "I think you're interested."

"I'm going to combust—"

He shifted to his knees. "Just lift your hips—but don't put pressure on your ankle."

I was already raising my ass so he could slide my pants over my hips.

He yanked my underwear down as well—mindful of my cock, thank God. Then, finally, he palmed my shaft. He grasped it and gave a playful tug.

I groaned as a drip of precum leaked.

He lapped it up, scraping his tongue along my sensitive slit.

My hips jerked.

His gaze met mine as he swallowed me down.

*I'm a goner.*

# Chapter Eight

Ethan

*He tastes even better than I imagined.*

After all the fated-mates stories I'd heard at Gran's knee, I hadn't been certain what would happen when I met mine.

I swallowed him down again, taking him to the back of my throat.

His hips jerked.

I nearly choked, but was able to move back in time.

"Sorry." Kingston said the word through gritted teeth.

*Poor man.*

I speared his slit again, then swirled my tongue around his crown.

Another moan.

I drew him deeper into my mouth and raked my teeth gently against him.

"I'm coming."

That was the only warning I got as he shot hot cum down my throat. I swallowed as best I could, even as he continued pulsing in my mouth.

His breath was coming in short, sharp pants.

*Ha. I did that to him.*

Blow jobs were my specialty. Or so my various hookups said. And I had no reason to doubt them.

Kingston softened in my mouth.

I swallowed one last time, pressed a kiss to his flaccid dick, and then crawled up his side until I could give him a kiss. A tongue-thrust-in-mouth down'n'dirty kiss.

He grasped my hair and held me in place as he fucked my mouth with his tongue.

*I can't wait for him to fuck my ass. It'll be so damn good.*

For now, though, his cock was exposed to the chilly air, and I didn't want him getting cold. Reluctantly, I pulled back.

Glazed gray eyes met mine.

"Blanket."

"Oh." Slowly, he nodded.

I tucked him back into his briefs and, with his help, put his pants back over his hips. I pulled the blanket over him and tucked him in.

"You?" His glassy eyes were unfocused.

"I'm good."

"No, I mean—"

"I know what you mean. Reciprocity is not required. I just want you to have a good nap."

"Cuddle with me?" He closed his eyes. "No one's every cuddled with me before. No one's ever made me feel the way you have before."

I wanted to ask him which way, but he was already drifting.

So I arranged the blanket over both of us and curled into his side.

In rest, he put his arm around me and pulled me closer. For a guy who claimed he didn't do this, he was doing a pretty damn good job.

I pressed the heel of my hand to my cock—willing it to deflate.

*Blue balls never killed anyone. Being here is way more important than an orgasm.* And since I hadn't slept at all last night, I closed my eyes and fell asleep as well.

Hours later, a buzzing pulled me from my reverie.

My ass was vibrating.

Okay, not in a good way.

I snagged Kingston's phone from my back pocket and held up the screen.

It showed me a text, but not the actual message.

*Damn.*

"Babe?"

He groaned.

"This might be important."

His eyes popped open. Clearly he was disoriented, and confused, because he blinked several times while staring at me.

I held his phone up.

He snagged it, entered a passcode, and stared. He cleared his throat. "Well...this is interesting."

I perked. I liked *interesting*. "Uh-huh. What?"

"Tabitha and Gillian are amending their request and asking us to join them tonight. Apparently, they want us to meet their friend, Kat."

"That sounds like fun. I'm always up to meeting new people."

He squinted at me, as if trying to figure out some great mystery.

I poked his ribs. "She threatened to tell Hallstein. Like, so you need to go. Right?"

"You don't even know who Hallstein is."

"Nope." I grinned. "But you do. And the guy's important. So text her that we'll see her at whatever time and which dessert can we bring? Or wine? Or salad?"

His nose wrinkled. He typed out a message with his index finger.

So cute.

I was a proficient two-thumb texter.

His phone buzzed again. "She said dessert would be lovely."

"Great. Peanut brittle and some kind of cheesecake with fresh fruit."

"Together?" He wrinkled his nose.

"No. As two things."

"We'll stick to just cheesecake. I don't think peanut brittle counts as a dessert."

After a moment, his phone buzzed again. "Six o'clock. Casual." He sighed as he dropped the phone to his chest—an entire three inches. "What have I done?" That came out on a moan.

"Accepted a dinner invitation from two lovely women." I scooted out of bed. "I need to feed you lunch now so you're not hangry when we get to their place. Something light. Oh, bean salad."

"Just no pineapple, okay?"

"Ew. Even I know you don't mix pineapples and beans. Well—"

"Go, Ethan." He gave me a scowl, but his voice was laced with amusement.

Four hours later, we sat in Tabitha and Gillian's beautifully appointed living room. While this room was quite formal, the tour of the rest of the house had shown a well-loved home where the women clearly enjoyed their lives together.

*So sweet.*

Kat, however, was a different story.

At first, I'd thought Gillian and Tabitha wanted to set Kingston up with Kat.

Which would've been cute. *Double K.*

Except from all the little comments Tabitha made, clearly she believed Kingston, and I were together. Which we were. But we hadn't been two days ago. So that part confused me.

Kingston and I sat on a rather uncomfortable couch. Gillian and Tabitha sat on a love seat, holding hands.

Super adorable.

Kat leaned against the fireplace and set her gaze on me.

After a long moment, Kingston scooted closer and took my hand.

I appreciated the support.

Kat examined her claws.

Oops. Fingernails. Really, really, really long fingernails.

Finally, she cleared her throat. "I'm going to provide you with the opportunity to amend your previous story. The one about how you found Tabitha's keys." She eyed the other woman.

Who straightened her spine. "Kat."

Kat offered a laissez-faire shrug.

Tabitha pursed her lips.

Her friend returned her laser-intense focus to me.

This time, I cleared my throat. "It's like I said—"

"No, it's not like you said. Bluebell's owner brought homemade cookies to apologize for the hassle."

"Oh, what kind? My favorite is peanut brittle. Although that isn't really a cookie. It's a sweet treat. And not everyone can have it, right? Because of peanut allergies. Although they've discovered that if you expose people who are allergic to just a taste every day that eventually they're, like, cured or something. I can find the study. Truly fascinating. Because, let's be honest, being allergic to peanuts would suck. Isn't peanut butter just the best food ever? Invented right here in Canada. Oh, or did she bring sugar cookies? Those are Kingston's favorite. Especially vanilla-flavored. I wanted to bring those tonight, but Kingston said we had to go elegant, and that was cheesecake and, of course, fresh fruit on the top. Can I have the kiwi slice? Oh, and can Kingston have the strawberry? He just loves berries..."

I didn't yelp when Kingston squeezed my hand—but it was a damn close thing.

Kat blinked. Several times. Finally, she gave a little shake of her head. Her gorgeous mane of blonde hair shimmered in the firelight.

Gas fires weren't good for the environment, but Gillian assured me they only used it for special occasions and when the weather was super chilly out.

Like tonight.

More cold rain forecasted.

"Okay." Kat let out a long breath. "What kind of shifter are you?"

Kingston's grip on my hand tightened.

I glanced at him.

He met that gaze and gave me a quick shake of his head.

"Oh, Mr. Locksmith, the question goes for you as well." She blew on her nails, then flexed her fingers.

"Holy shit."

All eyes turned to look at me.

"You're a lioness shifter." So damn obvious now I had a moment of clarity.

Her cat eyes glinted.

Kingston drew in a sharp breath.

She waved him off. "I'm not going to shift. I'd destroy the furniture and my best friend would kill me."

"So would her wife." Gillian arched an eyebrow at the queen of the land before focusing her attention on me. "I am, apparently, the only non-shifter in the room."

I gaped. "But you know?"

Kat snickered. "My bestie was so besotted that she couldn't keep a secret. Well, I might've also given her permission." She pivoted her attention to me. "But the rule about humans not finding out about us stands. How you've managed to keep the secret for twenty years is beyond me."

"Hey!"

She arched an eyebrow.

"I'm twenty-four."

"Still a baby."

Yet I didn't figure she was that much older than me. Still... "Squirrel."

Tabitha guffawed.

Even the quelling look from Kat didn't put a dent in her obvious amusement. "Oh, that's priceless. Of course you found my keys."

"Hey, that was hard work."

"And our poor neighbor is completely mystified." Gillian didn't appear quite as amused.

"Oh." I winced.

Kat waved me off. "Tabitha told Fania she'd mentioned seeing Bluebell, and you'd put two and two together and decided there must be a thieving dog in the neighborhood. Fania's promised to keep better track of her wayward dog."

This time, Kingston snickered. "Oh, cute."

All three women turned to him.

"Amusing?" Kat cocked her head, again flexing her fingers like claws.

Kingston swallowed. Hard. Yet his gaze never faltered. "Racoon."

Gillian wagged her finger. "Is it true racoons can open locks?"

"I'm going to say urban legend because, even if true, I'd never give away my species' secrets." He jutted his chin at Tabitha.

"Owl." She grinned.

I nearly bounced off the couch. "Oh God, do you belong to a parliament of owl shifters? I mean, how cool is that? Okay, maybe not as much as a pride—" I nodded to Kat. "—but still really neat. And you can't shift while you're pregnant, right? Because—" I winced. "Hey!" Finally, I glared at Kingston. He didn't have to squeeze my hand so hard I was certain circulation was cut.

Tabitha laughed. "Yes, that's true." She patted her flat stomach. "The reason we're not having a shifting party in the basement. I don't like to be left out. FOMO is a thing."

Gillian rolled her eyes. "And yes, I'm going to be a mother to owl-shifter babies. That's...mind-blowing."

"You'll help them embrace their human side." Kat's eyes softened. Then she pivoted her attention back to me. "You need to be more careful."

"But—"

She glared.

I shrank.

A bit.

Kingston cleared his throat. "In his defense—"

"Was I speaking to you?" Kat growled.

"Uh...no, ma'am." He shrank just that little bit as well. Normally he was self-possessed and strong. In the face of a lioness, though, he knew better. She'd eat him for a snack, spit out the bones, and then go find a coyote *and* bear for dinner.

"So, Squirrel..."

"Yes?" I perked.

"You're going to be more careful. None of this almost getting caught. You do what humans do. I can't believe, at—" She waved her hand around.

"Twenty-four."

"—twenty-four, that you haven't learned this most important lesson."

"Oh no, I know. Gran tells me all the time. Just..." I shrugged, trying to find the right words. "I could help. Why would I not help?"

"Because discovery is more important than getting a few locks changed." Her gaze settled on Tabitha.

"I blame Bluebell." She shrugged. "But I'll be more careful in the future."

Gillian raised her hand. "I didn't have lunch, and I'm starving. If we're done with the whole blaming and shaming and lecturing, could we eat?"

I liked her. Enough gumption to stand up to the lioness. "Have you ever—"

She shot me an amused look. "Yes, I've seen them both shifted. They run up near Whistler sometimes. I get to hang around and watch their clothes. I look forward to having a baby to occupy my time." She pressed her hand to Tabitha's belly.

Kat blew out a long breath. "You always manage to undermine me."

"You started it." Gillian met her stare.

I cocked my head.

Tabitha grinned. "My favorite troublemakers. Do you want to start with dessert? I can see you salivating for the kiwi slice." She favored Kingston with a smile. "And berries, eh? Should've guessed racoon right away."

Which signaled the end of the confab.

Dinner proved to be absolutely delightful as we touched on a range of topics from politics—human and shifter—to philosophy and religion. Then we moved to entertainment. Gillian recounted her adventures as a contestant on *Finding Love in All the Right Places*. I'd watched the lesbian dating show last year. I should've recognized her right away, but my mind hadn't gone there. I'd been too obsessed Friday night with keys and tonight with not being eaten by a lioness.

Kat butted into the conversation by adding that Tabitha had been the executive producer and extremely jealous of the other women's interest in Gillian—whom she perceived as *hers*.

Both women shot glares at Kat.

*There's a story here. I'm not going to ask...but I am going to search on the internet when I get home tonight...assuming I'm not having fun with Kingston.*

Kingston who never watched reality television and didn't have a clue what we were talking about.

I said we'd watch.

Gillian begged us not to, saying she was a different person now.

Since she hadn't known shifters existed before being on the show, then I had to agree with that.

We didn't eat the cheesecake first, instead enjoying a meal of vegetarian lasagna—with a side of steak for Kat—and asparagus with cheese sauce.

I chatted the entire drive home as Kingston stared moodily at the streetlamps.

Only when we were safely in the garage, did I venture to say what was really on my mind. "Are you ashamed of me?"

"What?" He scowled. "Why would you say that?"

"Because you didn't tell them. That we're mates."

He sputtered out a laugh. "Uh, dear Ethan. You went on at least thirty monologues—"

"Hey!"

"—don't interrupt."

I harrumphed.

"And you didn't say anything either. I kept waiting for you to just spill the beans...but you didn't. I figured you must've had a good reason."

"I was, uh, trying to be discreet...?"

Another laugh. "Indiscreet is your middle name. You don't know how to keep your mouth shut. As Kat asked, how *did* you get to be twenty-four without telling the human world about shifters?"

"Uh..." I scrunched my nose. "Because Gran asked me not to. I might be a *continual disappointment* to my dad, but I never want Gran to be upset with me."

"Your dad doesn't always sound like a nice man. In fact, I can't remember you saying very much that's nice about him."

"Oh." I frowned. "Well...huh." More thought. "He's not a *bad* man. Just set in his ways. You saw tonight."

"Saw what?"

"Squirrels are close to the bottom of the pecking order." I scratched my nose. "I mean, mice and rats are lower, but generally rodents are near the bottom. We only rank a bit above because we're so pretty." I tucked my hands under my chin and batted my eyelashes.

He sighed. "It's still not right. And I didn't see it tonight—that the women treated you as lesser than. I think I more noticed how we all deferred to Kat."

"Except Gillian."

"Yeah, you noticed that too, eh? She's seen Kat in her lioness form and still doesn't cower."

"What do you think it would be like to cuddle with a lioness shifter?"

He barked out a laugh. "Well, unless you have a hankering to do it, I doubt Kat would be interested."

My eyes widened. "Not me." I pressed a hand to my chest. "I meant, like, anyone who chooses Kat as a partner. Does she...I mean, would she need to end up with a lion shifter? And, while we're asking questions...how did a lioness shifter wind up in Vancouver? British Columbia? Canada?"

"I honestly don't know. If we ever see her again, you're free to ask her." He grinned.

"Which you know will never happen."

"Our paths might cross—"

"I mean that I'll never have the guts to ask her."

"Ah, but I might." He held my gaze. "Come to bed?"

"With pleasure."

# Chapter Nine

Kingston

His easy acquiescence—and acceptance—that he was coming to my bed made things simple. I wasn't letting him go.

Ever.

Twenty minutes later, we were in bed.

Naked.

He'd propped up my sore ankle and made a hot chocolate with milk so I could take an anti-inflammatory. His inherent nature was also to nurture. On the way home, he'd mentioned just a few of the many, many, many jobs he'd had in the past six years—plus a few he'd held in high school to earn pocket money. The list had made my head spin.

But somewhere in there had been line cook in a fancy restaurant. In the end, he'd clashed with the head chef over the right way to make a peanut drizzle.

No surprise there.

He used that experience, though, to make meals for those he cared about. He proudly informed he that he'd stocked my pantry full of spices and staples, and I'd be eating healthy for, uh, the rest of my life.

I might've confessed my cholesterol numbers had been trending in the wrong direction, my iron levels were low, and my blood sugar was a little high. I cared about these things—just not enough to change my eating habits.

My garbage eating habits.

According to Ethan.

He grinned at me. "What are you thinking?"

I finished off the last of the hot chocolate. I put the mug on the nightstand, then I met his gaze. "That I don't understand how I got to be so lucky."

His blue eyes shone with happiness. "Because you went for a run and found your mate." He caressed my cheek. "I know I'm a lot. Gran says that all the time."

"When do I meet your gran?" I didn't want him disparaging himself. That I'd been so cruel the other day in essentially telling him to shut up shamed me. He just...had a different way of communicating. Perhaps, in an appropriate moment, we could have the *time and place* discussion. But I didn't want to clip his wings. I wanted him to fly. Well, at least from tree to tree.

Not like Tabitha's owl. I'd leaving the soaring to her.

Although she'd offered to take Ethan for a ride.

To my relief, he'd declined.

"I'd love for you to meet Gran. Maybe we can invite her over? And I can cook something that appeals to both of you. She's pretty easygoing. She just..." He blinked a couple of times. "I'm going to miss living near her."

"Would you want her to move in with us?" *Now I'm the one who's a little loopy.* But the idea felt right. Like this was something we needed to do.

He bit his lip? "Really?"

"Yes. I have that room at the back of the house, so she wouldn't have to worry about stairs. We can set it up however she likes."

"She can help us raise our children."

The needle on the old record player I'd inherited from my father screeched on my favorite Billy Joel album. "Say what?"

"Well, you need a child to carry on your legacy. What will happen to your business?"

"I was going to sell it..." I said the words slowly. The first time, in my life, that I'd uttered them aloud.

"Nope. You need a child to carry on the family tradition. Now, I'm hoping you won't care if it's a boy or girl—"

"I don't." The job could be done by anyone willing to learn. A young woman might face some discrimination...but hopefully by the time she was an adult, some of that would have dissipated. Things were already better in the twenty years I'd done this job. "You make it sound so simple."

"Well..." He scrunched his nose. "We need to find a racoon-shifter surrogate. That's going to be tough. But there's a website."

"You've looked."

"Of course. I mean, I want kids and didn't want a wife. I mean, unless she turned out to be my fated mate in which case I wouldn't have had a choice."

"We don't have to have a racoon kit. We could always have a squirrel pup."

His eyes glistened with tears. He swallowed. Hard. "Maybe one of each?"

I couldn't think of anything that sounded sweeter. "I'd...be honored." I rubbed my nose. "But isn't this..."

"Too soon? Probably. I mean, I was hoping you'd fuck me tonight, but talking about our future is even more important. We need to know where we're headed, I think."

"Well, I want you to move in. You can put your stuff wherever you want. We can donate whatever of our things no longer work for us. We have three other rooms up here—so, as time moves on—we can turn them into rooms for our kids." Now, I swallowed hard. "Gran can move in downstairs, if she wants, and we'll have our family." I sniffed. "That sounds too easy."

"Gran said when she met Gramps, she knew. And they had a good, long life together. His heart attack was because of a genetic issue. Neither my dad nor I have it. So...I should probably live a long life as well. Once your health is better, you can anticipate that as too."

Shifter genetics allowed us to live longer, healthier lives. My parents dying in their seventies was unusual.

Ethan was right. From this moment forward, I needed to take care of myself. "Okay."

He did a little bouncy thing on the bed.

*This is too easy. He's going to get bored. He's going to find someone younger. Someone more attractive. Someone to hold his interest.*

I tried to quiet the voice of doubt in my head. Yes, those things were possible. Or, perhaps, I could keep the Ethan of this moment. And if his gran moved in, then he'd have to stay.

Right?

Right.

Slowly, he moved toward me. He put his hands on either side of my head on the pillow and moved toward me.

*I can't wait. We've never made love. We're about to embark on a life together...and we've never made love.*

Ethan appeared to have had the same realization as his eyes flashed when he moved in for a kiss. His soft lips touched mine, and I nibbled. He used that opportunity to thrust his tongue into my mouth.

He was a damn good kisser. Much better than I was. I shoved aside the thought that he'd likely had a lot more practice than myself. I could either be jealous of everyone who had come before, or enjoy the fact my mate knew how to...

*Oh holy hell.*

My cock jerked as his hand encircled it and squeezed.

He pulled back. "Lube?"

"Top drawer." I waved in the general direction of the nightstand.

He grinned as he reached over me to open the drawer and grab it. "I'm going to ride you so hard."

"Uh, okay." I'd sort of assumed we'd have to wait until my ankle healed. If he was careful, though, this would work. I'd just have to lie back and enjoy myself.

I could totally do that.

Within moments, he'd pulled back the covers, coated his fingers with lube, and prepped himself.

"One day...I want to do that."

He grinned. "Oh, count on it. But for tonight? I can't wait." He groaned.

Then tossed me the lube.

With fumbling fingers, I coated my cock. The shaft that was already leaking a drop of precum. I wasn't going to think about just how long it'd been since I'd been with someone.

"Okay, ready?" Ethan's face was alight with glee.

I'd never get tired of gazing at that smile.

"Yes, I'm ready."

"Hang on, it's going to be a wild ride."

*I don't doubt that. Every minute with you, I'm going to have to stay on my toes.*

With great care, he positioned himself with his calves on either side of my hips, then he crouched, held my cock in place, and slowly lowered himself.

Warmth and tightness greeted me. I gritted my teeth as my crown breached him.

He grinned. Then he took his time, gently sliding up and down until he was finally seated.

My patience was beyond strained. My willpower nonexistent. My ability to hold out in question. "Now?" *Jesus, please say* yes. *I'll die if you don't—*

"Yep." He pressed his hands against my abs and began to raise and lower himself on me.

The tightness enveloping my cock had me seeing stars. Pleasure suffused my body as he worked his magic on me.

He moaned, and I noticed his cock jutting out.

With my lubed fingers, I grasped it.

"Yes, babe. Please." He elongated the word as he continued to ride me hard—as he'd promised.

I matched his rhythm with my tugs. Not too hard...but not too soft, either. He needed to feel well-used by the time this adventure was finished.

We came together like we'd been meant to. All who'd come before paled into the sepia of the past. He was all bright colors, shiny rainbows, and red glory.

A flush ran up his chest from his nipples to the tips of his ears. His breaths came in short, sharp pants as he worked himself on my cock.

He looked glorious as he arched his neck backward and said, "I'm coming, babe."

Not normally a fan of pet names, I found this one adorable. I redoubled my efforts to bring him to climax and, within moments, he spurted over my hand.

His inner walls battered my cock, and as I grasped his thighs, my balls drew up, and I surged within him as I came.

Hard.

He held still as I poured my cum into his ass.

*This is hotter than hell. Oh God...the look on his face.*

His bright-blue eyes held me mesmerized in their depths. He was my everything, and I didn't know how I'd live without him.

I said a quick prayer that I never would have to. I didn't believe in deities, but I believed in Mother Earth—and so I placed my request to her that she always care for my Ethan.

He eased off me, and I slipped from him with a little squelching noise. The bed could be a mess, but—

"I'm going to get a washcloth so I can clean us off. Nothing less appealing than cum-covered sheets." He was up and gone before I could respond.

Resting my hand on my belly, I awaited his return.

He popped into the room from the ensuite and quickly poked his head into the walk-in closet. "I suspect I'm doing laundry tomorrow." He moved toward me. His eyes were alight as he'd obviously spotted my pile of dirty clothes.

"Well..."

"I don't mind. I can make vegetarian lasagna while I do all the messy uniforms piled in that room."

"I..."

"My pleasure, okay? I like to keep a clean nest."

"And yet when you cook, you use every pan, dish, and bowl in the place."

He grinned as he knelt on the bed. "But I always clean everything up."

"You have me there." I sighed as he ran the washcloth over my belly and grinned when he thoroughly cleaned my flaccid cock. "That's lovely."

"I'll always take care of you." He pressed a kiss to my lips, then scurried back to the bathroom. Moments later, he returned. He pulled the blankets over us—mindful of my ankle—and settled against my side.

I ruffled his hair as a feeling of pure contentment—unlike anything I'd ever felt before—settled over me.

*Thanks, Mom and Dad. You promised this would happen, and you were right. I'm sorry I'd given up hope. I'll be the best mate I can possibly be. That, I pledge to you.* I probably should've pledged those words to Ethan as well, but his breaths had already lengthened and his body slackened.

He was asleep.

A long time passed before I joined him.

## Chapter Ten

Ethan

Even I was amazed at how easily we settled into a routine. Of the thirty-five callouts we did in the next three weeks, I found keys for nine of them.

I worried Kingston would be mad because I was taking away his business, but he simply beamed with pride. And most of the grateful owners of the found keys gave us big tips because of the money and hassle we saved them.

Finding keys was easy.

Keeping up with Kingston's mood swings was getting easier.

Convincing Gran to move in with us was tougher.

She carried on about how we needed to settle into our coupledom before she invaded.

Kingston kept repeating that we had the room set up for her, and he'd be honored if she made our home hers as well.

Gran was stubborn, though.

So I split my time between Kingston's house—well, now my place too—and spending time with Gran. I was getting tired, and I worried about both of them home alone for extended periods of time. She'd lived alone for years, but I'd always been right next door. Now I was miles away.

Kingston still tried to do everything, and the doctor wasn't happy with his progress.

Or lack thereof.

Gran tried to do everything herself and wound up scratching herself on the roses.

The two most important people in my life.

Stubborn as hell.

I sat in the kitchen one morning as my love scrolled on his phone. I hadn't *told* him that I loved him…yet. But my feelings had to be pretty damn clear to him. "Maybe if we held a dinner party?"

He raised his gaze to meet mine. And blinked. "Dinner party?"

"Yeah. We can invite Peter, Thomas, Skylar, and Samuel. Gran's a huge fan of Peter's—so she'll want everything to be perfect. If she comes over to help, then she'll see what a great house you have and how her bedroom is so convenient and…" Because I'd yet to coerce—sorry, convince—Gran to visit.

Kingston had come with me several times to see her.

She'd been charmed.

And yet still had refused to come over.

"A dinner party? I don't do…dinner parties."

I clapped my hands. "Well, it's time to start. Having the Ericksons over for dinner is perfect." Well, Thomas and the kids went by his last name, not Peter's, and I couldn't remember what that was. They'd made the decision so the kids would have a prayer of not always being known as *Peter Erickson's* children. He loved them, but he didn't want them saddled with fame.

Truthfully, I understood that.

"I don't know..." Kingston frowned.

"Well, we could invite Hallstein and Myles as well." I had yet to meet the couple, but they sounded adorable. "Oh, and Kat, Gillian, and—"

"No." He shook his head. "The women *or* the studio people."

"But Tabitha *is* a studio person."

"Yes, but the Walshes, Hallstein, and Myles aren't shifters. I think..." He frowned.

"Ha! You're considering it." I pumped my fist in the air.

He glowered.

For two-point-six seconds.

"Separate. So pick one or the other. The Walshes might be busy, you know. Peter's in demand—"

"They're available Friday. Hallstein said he and Myles would be thrilled to attend, and they're bringing the best Caesar salad ever." I scrunched my nose. "I think mine's pretty good, but I'm happy to fawn over someone else's. Gran agreed we should make one vegetarian and one meat dish. We're still debating what the kids should—"

Kingston waved his hand in the air, effectively silencing me.

"Wait."

"Uh...okay..."

"You've already invited everyone?"

"Well, I didn't invite Kat, Gillian, and Tabitha. I thought of the whole mixing shifters and non-shifters thing. I figured I'd leave that up to you. Personally, I know this amazing buck shifter who I think would be perfect for Kat—"

He waved his hand again.

I sighed

"You're thinking of setting up a lioness shifter with a buck shifter?"

"Of course. I mean, I guess she could eat him. But she didn't eat us, and we're so much easier on the digestive—"

He closed his eyes, and let out a long sigh. "So you're telling me Hallstein, Myles, Peter, Thomas, and the two kids are coming...?"

"Friday night."

"Friday night." He repeated the words for size. "And today is...?"

"Wednesday." *How does he not know what day it is? He's so obsessive about these*— "Oh."

"Yes, oh. These things take time to plan—"

"I thought you said you didn't do dinner parties."

His mouth slammed shut.

"Gran is coming over this afternoon. The delivery will be here within an hour, so she'll have everything she needs. If I'm not out on a call with you, then I'll help her. You're sitting back and reclining and enjoying the fragrant smells permeating your home."

That, at least, brought a smile to his face. His old high-back chair had a new home in the living room, and we'd installed a recliner in the family room. He was now able to raise his ankle without having to use his coffee table—which had driven him nuts to do.

I rose. "I forgot to tell you that I found a neat little store nearby that has a great selection of fruits and vegetables."

He sighed.

Undaunted, I continued. "Anyway, I just had to stop." I moved to the fridge. "Look what they had. Raspberries. You like raspberries, right? And I found sour plums. I remember my friend Jake getting drunk on them. Who knew that was a thing?"

"My friend Luigi ate too many that one time. He got so drunk he fell out of the tree. Bad back sprain. He was able to shift, though. Swore he'd never eat them again."

"Well, you're only going to have one or two."

"I didn't—"

"Just the raspberries this morning." I had washed them thoroughly before putting them in a bowl. I handed him that and a fork.

"Don't I get whipped cream?"

"If you're good today, we can have whipped cream tonight."

The doorbell buzzed.

"In bed." I darted from the room and made it to the front door quickly. I opened the door to find one of the handsomest men I'd ever met standing before me. He wore a green-and-black uniform and had a wide grin on his beautiful face. "Grocery delivery for Ethan?"

"Yep. That's me." I eyed the bins he'd piled on the front porch. "Let me grab some bags—"

"I can bring these in the house—"

"Oh no. No shoes."

"I can remove—"

"Really, I'll be right back." I closed the door and headed to the closet in the laundry room where we kept the cloth bags.

I returned to find Kingston peeking out the front window—toward the porch. "What are you doing?"

"He's very attractive."

"Yeah...okay..." I pulled four bags out from a larger one, giving me five good ones to work with.

"Is he gay?"

I blinked. "How on earth would I know? I don't generally ask the sexual orientation of my delivery drivers. I do want them to come back instead of going back to their companies, making legitimate complaints about sexual harassment, and then getting us blacklisted."

"Well…when you put it like that—"

"I'm gay and very taken."

The young man's voice rang clear.

Damn. I hadn't closed the front door all the way. "Uh, sorry." I opened the front door. "My boyfriend's just…"

"Jealous?"

I held up my thumb and forefinger a quarter of an inch apart.

Hunky delivery driver arched an eyebrow.

I held them an inch apart. "We're new."

"Well, congrats. I hope things go well." He snagged the biggest bag and quickly filled it with fruits and vegetables.

I hauled the sack of potatoes inside and then returned to get the two jugs of milk.

By then, he had most of the dry goods in another bag and was starting on the dairy products.

Kingston had a thing for cheese.

Go figure.

Within a couple of minutes, I had everything loaded into the house and the cute guy was backing his delivery van out of the driveway and was headed south.

I went back in the house and wiped my feet on the mat. They were nearly frozen, but I hadn't had time to don socks or shoes. "I need to get slippers."

"I'll buy you a pair."

After a moment, I pursed my lips. "Jealousy? Honestly, Kingston, it doesn't look good on you. I mean, I guess I should be flattered, but—"

"You're right." He winced as he continued to balance on his crutches. "I just…" He sighed. "I've never dated anyone as attractive as you before. And people look. As they should. But I want to snatch you away and say *hands off, he's mine.*"

"Oh, babe. I *am* yours. I live here. I want Gran to move in with us. Would someone who wasn't committed do those things?"

Indecision warred on his face. He'd never said anyone had hurt him—had betrayed him. But then, as he had admitted, he'd never dated anyone seriously. Feelings had never become entrenched. He'd never enmeshed himself into someone else's life.

I advanced on him, then ran my index finger down his chest. "You're my fated mate. Now, are we good?"

"Uh, yeah."

"Great. Let's get cracking. Or, uh, putting groceries away."

We did.

Well, I did, and he supervised.

Then Gran came over.

Kingston and I had only a few callouts and so, by Friday night—without things to occupy his time—he was going out of his mind.

I did convince him to tussle with me in the backyard Thursday around midnight—in our animal forms, of course.

By the end, he was breathless, happy, and we made love under the full moon.

On a heated blanket, but we still froze our asses off and, totally zero regrets.

"Christmas is coming soon." Gran pulled her famous dinner rolls out of the oven as I checked to make certain the honey butter was the perfect consistency.

"I know. Mom's asked me to bring Kingston for Christmas dinner." I tapped my fingers on the counter, holding back the urge to ask Gran—again—if she'd move in. As a Christmas present to me.

"I think that's a lovely idea. I don't understand why you're reticent. Your mother's thrilled you've met your fated."

My nose twitched at the fresh-baked smell. "Dad's not, though."

"Well..." She put her hand on her hip. "My son's a stubborn one. He...thought you'd carry on the lineage."

"I've been looking into squirrel-shifter surrogates. It would be my sperm."

"Yes, but..."

"He envisioned me bringing home a beautiful squirrel to complete the picture. Not a grumpy racoon."

She laughed. "He does have his moments."

"Oh, Gran, he's so much better than he used to be. Of course, he puts on his best show for you—"

"I want him to be himself."

I tapped my chin. "A sex demon? Because, let me tell you—"

"Ethan." She swatted me with her oven mitt.

I laughed.

Kingston hobbled into the kitchen. "I heard laughing." He met Gran's gaze. "That always worries me."

She nodded solemnly. "Often, with my favorite grandson, that means trouble."

"Hey, I'm your only grandson." Despite squirrels being prolific maters, my parents only had me and my three younger—and as of yet still unmarried—sisters. Perhaps if one or more of them married and had pups of their own, my dad might stress less.

The doorbell buzzed.

Kingston and I had a *long* conversation about allowing socks, and maybe even shoes, in the house. He'd managed to keep his mouth shut with Gran and I trusted him to do the same with our guests.

# UNLOCKED AND UNLOST

I scooted to the front door and opened it to find Hallstein and Myles. A greater study in contrasts, I couldn't remember meeting.

Hallstein was very much like Kingston—black hair, dark-brown eyes and very serious.

With a black silk tie. Covered in neon Christmas balls.

Myles was far more like myself—a riot of color. With his white-blond hair, light-brown eyes, neon-green shirt that matched one of the Christmas balls, and a pair of red suede pants. He was also shorter than his husband by several inches.

I grinned as I held the door open for them.

To my surprise, Myles wrapped me in a warm hug. "We just knew Kingston was going to find the right person. He's come out of his shell so much."

I blinked, then gazed at Hallstein. He'd brought a small safe to the house a week back because the owner, a lovely actress named Elouise, had lost the key. Apparently, she'd been on set the day of the infamous janitor's closet incident, and just figured Hallstein could help.

His solution was to drop by our place. After having called first, of course.

I'd been doing laundry in the basement, and so had left Kingston and the security chief alone.

And now Hallstein's husband was claiming my mate had *come out of his shell?* "Uh, okay."

Hallstein smiled as he held a stainless-steel bowl. "He...spoke glowingly of you. I might've overshared with my dearest." He shot Myles what I'd term a warning glare.

Myles smiled, blew a kiss, toed off his shoes, grabbed the bowl, and headed toward the kitchen.

In his wake, Hallstein sighed. He bent to untie his laces.

"I love him." I couldn't help myself.

Hallstein shot up and nearly overbalanced. "Well, uh, he is quite...a lot."

I blinked.

He blinked.

"I meant Myles. In the platonic *I think he's so fab* sense."

"Ah." He nodded. "I also meant Myles. In the *yes, we're complete opposites and yet I can't imagine my life without him* sense. But I also think you and Kingston are perfect for each other. If Myles and I made it, you and Kingston can as well."

On impulse, I went up on my toes to press a kiss to his cheek. "Thank you."

Before he could answer, the doorbell buzzed.

"I'll just get out of your way."

"You know where the kitchen is."

Gran's laugher mixed with Myles's reached us.

"Ah, yes. Making friends wherever he goes." Hallstein saluted and headed toward the back of the house.

I opened the front door to find two of the most adorable creatures I'd ever beheld.

And their fathers.

Things were chaotic as we got coats, mitts, and boots off the kids.

Skylar, who was barely three, babbled and, although little made sense to me, she was clearly taken with my bow tie.

Samuel was a quiet one. He'd had some medical issues, as Thomas had explained to me, and was a little behind in normal infant progress. He wasn't crawling yet, and very much preferred to be carried by Peter.

The doctor said the little guy would find his footing eventually and that, for now, security and comfort were more important than some milestones.

Their daughter's mother had used drugs until she'd discovered she was pregnant, so Skylar's infancy hadn't been the easiest either. Now, though, she was a healthy toddler.

She escaped Thomas's grasp and followed the sound of voices.

He ran after her, muttering apologies.

I took a placid Samuel from Peter so he could at least take his coat and shoes off. He gave me a sheepish look.

"Relax. I love kids."

One of the sexiest men on the planet—according to people everywhere—offered me a genuine smile. "I'm so grateful for that."

I glanced behind me. "We're, uh…exploring our options." I turned back to Peter.

Slowly, he nodded. "I think it's a great idea. Thomas and I chose adoption because we found kids in need. Surrogacy is also an option."

"That's probably the route we'll take…" Because there didn't tend to be many orphan shifter children—although that did occasionally happen. We'd discussed it and, if we found a child in need, we wouldn't hesitate.

Yes, my Kingston had come a very long way.

"Skylar!" Thomas's warning was appreciated.

A blur of toddler nearly barreled into me.

I clung to Samuel while Peter scooped his daughter into his arms.

She squealed.

Thomas breathed a sigh of relief.

Myles poked his head through the archway. "Gran says wash your hands right now." He cocked his head. "And she's a little scary, so I wouldn't argue with her."

Peter frowned, but Thomas nudged his biceps. "Total joke. Gran's a sweetheart." He smiled at me. "Reminds me of my mother. Turns to mush around her grandkids."

That made me smile because I envisioned my grandmother doting on great-grandchildren. Oh, my mother would love my kids as well, but Gran was just...special. She had a way of making everyone feel they had a place in the world. That they were, in essence, as special as she was.

We all took turns in the powder room and soon, we all sat at the dining room table. At my insistence, Gran and Kingston each sat at the end. I positioned myself next to my mate and close to the kitchen so I could be the one to leap up if anything was missed.

Nothing had been.

The next hour was one of the best of my life. Everyone at the table contributed something unique. And all the adults took turns holding Samuel—who quite enjoyed the experience.

In the end, after dessert, Skylar took Myles on a *tour of the house* while the rest of us lounged and chatted.

Gran was in her element.

Kingston coped admirably.

None of us acted like having one of the biggest action movie stars on the planet dining with us was a big deal.

Said action star insisted on helping with the dishes—along with Hallstein and me.

Gran sat at the kitchen island and supervised.

And proclaimed, halfway through, that she was looking forward to moving in and *keeping an eye on my boys.*

Peter rescued the glass pan I nearly dropped.

I ran over and embraced her, uncaring of what anyone thought.

*See, I knew she'd come around.*

I couldn't wait to give her great-grandbabies. Or to introduce her to Kat, Gillian, and Tabitha.

# UNLOCKED AND UNLOST

After everyone, including Gran, had headed home, Kingston held me tight as we discussed how quickly we could move her in so she didn't have a chance to change her mind.

# Chapter Eleven

Kingston

I eyed Gran across the kitchen table.

She continued her knitting as she met my stare.

I sighed.

She smiled. "It's four days, Kingston, my dear. You can survive without my darling grandson for four days."

Arguing was pointless because I was the one who insisted Ethan go. His sister, Perla, needed a ride home from Kelowna, where she was attending the University of British Columbia Okanagan. He should've been able to do the trip in two days. Except for the snowstorm that hadn't been predicted. Waiting until the roads were clear before driving home was the best course of action.

I'd decided to take the weekend off.

That said, Peter had a driver on standby in case I needed her. A nice woman named Codi who worked for the studio. Apparently, she used to be a long-haul truck driver and could sling twenty-five-pound bags of sand like no one's business.

In other words, my tool kit wouldn't be an issue.

Unless I got an emergency call that I couldn't redirect, though, I was staying close to home. With Christmas just a week away, and with all Gran's festive baubles she'd collected over the last half-century decorating the house, sometimes I just liked to sit and admire the pretty.

The doorbell buzzed.

"I'll get it." She rose and hustled out of the room before I could move.

On her no-slip treaded slippers.

See? I could adapt. No way was I asking Gran to wash her feet and go barefoot in the house.

Ethan had quietly retired my buckets and had promised to wash the floors more frequently.

Which he had.

"Oh, Kingston, what a lovely surprise." Gran made her way over to me with...a pineapple?

Wrapped with decorative ribbon.

Okay.

I fingered the card attached. Finally, I opened it.

*Because I know you love these things. Missing you.*

"He seriously sent me a pineapple via delivery?"

"The man said it arrived in Vancouver this morning. From..." She frowned. "Hawaii? Does that sound right?"

"Hawaii does have pineapples."

She snatched it back. "Since it's fresh, let me chop it up right away."

The doorbell rang again.

"Oh dear." Gran had just sliced into the pineapple.

Much handier on the crutches than I'd been five weeks ago, I was up quickly. "I'll get it."

"Let me know if you need a hand, dear."

I hid my smile as I made my way to the front door. I adored that she called me *dear*. Reminded me of my mother and how affectionate she'd been.

On that thought, I opened the door.

To find a guy in a delivery outfit. He held a pizza box. "My friend Ethan said to bring you a pineapple pizza. Oh, I'm supposed to tell you there's ham as well, but to emphasize there's pineapple. Are you going to be able to carry..."

Gran bustled in behind me. "Thank you, Larry. So kind of you."

"Thanks, Gran. You take care." He scurried away.

I shut the door and turned to Gran.

She shrugged. "One of Ethan's friends growing up. Yes, squirrel shifter. Loves driving his muscle car all over town way too fast." She headed back toward the kitchen.

I followed.

And was barely seated when the doorbell buzzed again.

Gran headed back toward the front door.

Two minutes later, she was back with a bakery box that she presented to me.

Pineapple upside-down cake.

With another note.

*I miss you. See you soon.*

"Well, we'll have pizza for lunch and cake with fresh pineapple for dessert."

"But I don't like pineapple."

Gran patted my shoulder. "Nice try, dear. You graze on it every time Ethan presents it to you. He brought you those berries as well."

"I didn't ask where he found them."

"Probably best." She took the cake box from me. "As long as you wash them well, you'll be fine."

*Right.*

We ate the pizza, fresh pineapple, and upside-down cake. We watched *Vigilante Justice*. Thomas was a producer for the show and, as Ethan had said, the lead actor was a dreamboat. Cole Hamilton had starred in a movie with Peter a number of years ago—the show where Peter and Thomas had met on set.

In honor of their love match, Gran and I watched that movie after dinner.

We both might've required tissues. Sometimes even movies with happy endings brought tears.

Or so Gran assured me.

And we agreed Peter had absolutely deserved to win the Academy Award that year.

Just like Cole deserved to win the Golden Globe for *Vigilante Justice* this year.

Thanks to Gran and Ethan, I was getting caught up on all the productions in Vancouver I'd missed over the last...well, most of my life since I'd never paid attention to such things.

The next day I had one callout and, as promised, Codi with an *i* drove me to and from the site as well as hauled around my gear. The woman was an absolute hoot.

I still missed Ethan.

In the end, he was gone five days since the RCMP closed the Coquihalla Connector because of the nearly four feet of snow.

Eventually, though, he came home.

I knew this because of my doorbell.

*Buzz.*

*Buzz.*

*Buzz.*

*Buzz.*

Gran was home to greet Perla, so I was home alone and had to hobble to the door.

I threw open the door and grinned.

He grinned back. He stepped inside, dropped his overnight bag, shut the door, toed off his shoes, and then grabbed my cheeks. "Oh, babe, I missed you something fierce."

"Yeah?"

"Yeah."

We pressed our lips together in a toe-curling kiss. He deepened it, thrusting his tongue into my mouth.

My cock twitched.

*Down, boy. Surprises first. Sex later.*

The damn thing wasn't happy...but it complied.

"Okay." I rebalanced myself. "I have three surprises for you."

He blinked. "For me?"

Since he was always giving me surprises and not the other way around, I nodded. I was a little slow on the uptake, but I got there eventually. "First surprise is in my pocket."

"Oh, I think I like the sound of this." Said absolutely salaciously.

"Down, boy." Echo of the words I'd just said to my cock.

Who still wasn't happy, but was still at least complying.

Ethan slid his hand into my pocket and tilted his head when his fingers came into contact with his surprise. He withdrew a keychain and held it aloft between the two of us. "Uh, babe, you already gave me a key to the house."

"Yes, but I didn't give you a key to the van. And to the workshop. You'll need them."

"Okay." He grinned and his bright-blue eyes shone with happiness. He knew how much this meant to me.

"Second gift. Come to the basement with me."

"Great, I can bring my laundry as well." He slung the bag over his shoulder and waited for me to hobble my way down.

"I see the doctor tomorrow. I've been doing the weight-bearing exercises, and I should get the green light." Never would I be so happy. I'd followed all the rules and done all the physiotherapy—and still the ankle had taken unusually long to heal.

"You know I don't mind carrying your equipment around."

No missing the amusement in Ethan's voice.

"Codi did a pretty good job."

"So you said in your text. Do I need to worry?"

"No." I sighed with relief when I got to the bottom of the stairs. "She's very happy with her job at the studio. Okay, open the door." I pointed to the one leading to the big, cavernous space that I'd pretty much ignored for twenty years.

He cocked his head.

I gestured for him to do as I suggested.

He opened it, flipped on the light, and gasped. "Oh, Kingston."

"Yes. That's my name." Said as wryly as possible.

"You did this for me?"

"Yes." Again, with as much dry tone as I could inject.

"Oh wow."

He advanced into the room and I followed. I knew, of course, what he'd find.

Instead of the industrial-gray paint—drab, as Gran called it—the room shone with vibrant colors. The base coat was sunshine-yellow, but I'd had rainbows, meadows, forests, a sun, and all kinds of animals added.

One wall was midnight-blue with a moon throwing a glow over a rainforest.

An owl soared in silhouette against the moon.

*Tabitha will love that.*

Initially, I'd just planned bright colors. But then I thought about the kids we both wanted so badly. This room wasn't just for Ethan—although he was the genesis behind it. No, this room was for our family. A real *family* room.

"This is enormous."

"I hope you're talking about the television." I grinned. "Or my cock."

"Oh babe, you are so getting sucked tonight. I'd give you a blow job right now, but..."

"Yeah." I nudge him with my elbow. "This is family space."

"We've got the bedroom and the living room couch for fucking."

I wanted to object—but he might've ridden me mighty hard a couple of weeks ago.

Before Gran moved in, of course.

"Uh...not unless we're alone with no chance of visitors."

"Like tonight?"

I cocked my head. "Okay, yeah, like tonight. Although I have plans for us that involve a bed."

"Yippee." He threw his arms around my neck. "Best surprise ever. Truly."

"Well, I do have one more thing to share."

He waved his arm around the room. "I don't want anything else. This is...the best."

"I think I can do better. But if this is the high-water mark for the day, I'm fine with that." Because I'd never forget his look of pure, unadulterated joy at seeing this space. "Let's go to the garage."

"Okay, but let me put my laundry—"

"It'll keep. I'm certain your nasty underwear will still be here when we're done upstairs."

"Hey." Yet he grinned. "You first."

I made my way upstairs and into the garage.

Ethan turned on the light and stood, watching me. "Okay. Uh..."

I gestured to the side of the van with my chin.

And waited.

And waited.

Suddenly, tears filled his eyes and streamed down his face.

"No. No. No. Sweetheart, this was supposed to be a good surprise."

He sniffed. Then wiped his tears with his hands. "I...I don't know what to say."

"Well..." I swallowed. "Say *yes*. Say you'll do it."

He held my gaze before wrapping his arms around my neck. "Yes. A thousand times yes. Just...yes."

I blew out a breath. Mostly in relief—although partly in elation. "That's good because changing the van back would be a pain in the ass."

He laughed, breathing hot air against my neck.

"I have the paperwork for you to sign, and we'll let everyone know."

He pulled back. "I love you."

"I love you too. Just in case it wasn't super obvious."

He stepped away to lovingly caress the new logo on the van.

*Unlocked and Unlost.*

Together, we had it made.

*Epilogue*

Ethan

Five years.

Tomorrow, we, as a family, were going to have a big celebration with all our friends. Peter insisted because he still took credit as the matchmaker. We had so many people within our orbit—friends, family, colleagues...

Kingston pressed a kiss to my temple as we stood in our backyard—festooned with balloons, streamers, and a handmade sign reading *We Love You, Daddies!*

With the *a* in *Daddies* backward, of course.

Gran supervised, but she was judicious with her corrections.

Florence, our little kit, was mastering language just fine.

Sergio, our little pup, tended to be a step behind his sister. But he'd figured out scampering up trees quicker. His long red tail always helped for balance.

His sister liked to hoard things when she thought no one was watching. Then her brother would find them.

They'd been born within weeks of each other, ensuring absolute chaos in the house. But we hadn't wanted to wait once we'd found surrogates. Both Rachel, the racoon surrogate, and Stacey, the squirrel surrogate, had been thrilled to help us grow our family. Both had offered, in the past year, to help out again.

Kingston and I had decided, with no small amount of self-preservation, that two was perfect.

Oscar screeched and Olympia was at her brother's side in a moment. Tabitha and Gillian's twins were a year older than our two and had, almost from the moment they'd been born, been hell on wheels.

Being honorary godfathers, Kingston and I had a good sense of what we faced.

First crawl, first step, first shift... The dynamic duo taught us what to expect—enabling us to be better parents.

Or so we told ourselves.

Kingston pressed himself against my back.

I leaned into the embrace. "Is it me or is our life perfect?"

"Florence opened the wall safe."

I pulled away from him and gaped. "You said that safe was unbreakable. That was the entire point of having it installed." We kept all our important papers in there.

In the beginning, I'd helped with the business—mainly doing advertising and preparing papers for the accountant to file the tax returns.

When the kids, came, though, we decided I'd stay home with them. None of my jobs had even come close to the rewarding sense of guiding our two into their lives.

Gran showed me how.

I applied the lessons.

Kingston did as well, proving to be an amazing dad. He was the one who let the kids get away with way more than I would.

We were happy.

"Okay, you said that safe was uncrackable."

"It is."

"Yet our five-year-old broke into it? And she didn't use your drilling tools?"

"Nope."

I blinked back tears. "Our baby's growing up." I pressed a hand to my heart.

"What are you going on about now?" Kat pursed her lips. "I broke a nail."

"I'll get you a nail—" Kingston didn't even have a chance to finish the sentence before she had a file yanked from her pocket.

*Guess when you have nails like that, they might break more often.*

She'd proved a capable and competent aunt, teaching all the kids about how to stay safe while shifted. She watched over all of us.

I'd have thought it might feel stifling, but it really wasn't.

She treasured all the pups, kits, and owlets.

Gran clapped. "Cake."

Kingston groaned.

Food, no matter how delivered, meant a mess.

I kissed his cheek. "From the man who made me wash my feet, to dirty diapers, to messy faces."

"Oh God, don't remind me. I'm glad we said no more kids."

"Until we have grandkids." I tried to hide my smile.

He pressed a kiss to my lips. "I look forward to it."

I believed him. Because he had helped me find a purpose in life, and I'd unlocked his heart.

Want more Gabbi Grey?
Check out her film world books, set in beautiful Vancouver, British Columbia.
The books are:
Catch a Tiger by the Tail (Peter and Thomas)
Solstice Surprise (Peter and Thomas)
Valentino in Vancouver (Valentino and Seamus)
You See Me (Elouise and Kelci)
Sun, Surf, and Surprises (Alex and Jerome)
Ginger in the City (Adrian and Joel)
Caressa's Homecoming (Bound by Love Book 1) (Cole, Caressa, and Michael)
Cole's Reckoning (Bound by Love Book 2) (Cole, Caressa, and Michael)
Love On and Off the Set Boxset (including Myles and Hallstein) – coming 2026
Fly by Night Boxset (including Gillian, Tabitha, and Kat's stories) – coming 2026

Want Axel and Thornton's story?
Axe to Grind
Grindstone's Edge

Curious about Tarah and Sebastian? Check out this dark erotic BDSM (written as Gabbi Black)
Innocent Eyes

Want more?

Check out Gabbi's Love in Mission City series, set in beautiful British Columbia.

(Love in Mission City Book 1)
Stanley's Christmas Redemption (Love in Mission City Book 2)
The Beauty of the Beast (Love in Mission City Book 2.5)
Sleigh Bells and Second Chances (Love in Mission City Book 3)
A Daddy for Christmas 2: Foster (Love in Mission City Book 3.5)
Rayne's Return (Love in Mission City Book 4)
Gideon's Gratitude (Love in Mission City Book 5)
Love in Mission City: The Boyfriends Duet
Love in Mission City: The Shorts
Rayne Check
Archer's Awakening
Thought You Were the One
Love Without Reservations
The Lightkeeper's Love Affair
Ace's Place
Marcus's Cadence
Not in it for the Money

Also:

Axe to Grind
Grindstone's Edge
Hugh (Single Dads of Gaynor Beach)
Anthony (Single Dads of Gaynor Beach)
Xavier (Single Dads of Gaynor Beach)
Love Furever (Friends of Gaynor Beach Animal Rescue)
Husky Love (Friends of Gaynor Beach Animal Rescue)
Yorkie to My Heart (Friends of Gaynor Beach Animal Rescue)
My Past, Your Future

If Only for Today
Catch a Tiger by the Tail
Solstice Surprise
Valentino in Vancouver
You See Me
Sun, Surf, and Surprises
Ginger in the City
Caressa's Homecoming (Bound by Love Book 1)
Cole's Reckoning (Bound by Love Book 2)
An Uncommon Gentleman
A Sensible Gentleman
Didn't See You Coming
Finding Noah (Foggy Basin Season 2)
Unlocked and Unlost

Audiobooks
Ginger Snapping All the Way
Stanley's Christmas Redemption
Sleigh Bells and Second Chances
Rayne Check
Rayne's Return
Thought You Were the One
Love in Mission City: The Shorts
Page Against the Machine
The Lightkeeper's Love Affair
Ace's Place
Marcus's Cadence
Not in it for the Money
Hugh (Single Dads of Gaynor Beach)
Anthony (Single Dads of Gaynor Beach)

Love Furever (Friends of Gaynor Beach Animal Rescue)
My Past, Your Future
If Only for Today
Catch a Tiger by the Tail
Solstice Surprise
An Uncommon Gentleman
A Sensible Gentleman
Didn't See You Coming

Want a free short story? The story is set in Gaynor Beach, California where there are plenty of single dads and puppy rescues! You can sign up for my newsletter so you can keep up with all the great stuff I'm doing as well as pictures of my own pooches, Ally and Finnegan.
Hemingway's Happy Day

Love contemporary MF romances? What's better than love in the beautiful Cedar Valley in British Columbia, Canada? Find small town romances with a touch of angst, a bit of heat, and a lot of heart...
The Absolution of Abigail Reardon (prequel)
The Luminosity of Loriana Harper (Book 1)
The Making of Marnie Jones (Book 2)
The Redemption of Remy St. Claire (Book 3)

# Interested in knowing more about Gabbi?

Sign up for her newsletter
Follow her on Bookbub
Follow her on Instagram

USA Today Bestselling author Gabbi Grey lives in beautiful British Columbia where her fur baby chin-poo keeps her safe from the nasty neighborhood squirrels. Working for the government by day, she spends her early mornings writing contemporary, gay, sweet, and dark erotic BDSM romances. While she firmly believes in happy endings, she also believes in making her characters suffer before finding their true love. She also writes m/f romances as Gabbi Black and Gabbi Powell.

Made in the USA
Columbia, SC
27 May 2025